I0772225

A DARLING ARTIST

DARLING MEN
BOOK THREE

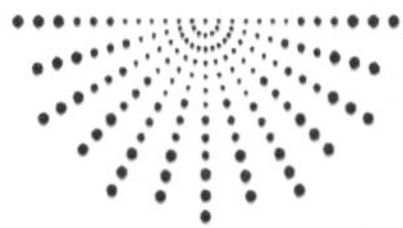

LARK HOLIDAY

GLASS ELEPHANT PRESS

A Darling Artist

Copyright © 2024 by Lark Holiday

All rights reserved.

No part of this book may be reproduced in any form or by any electronic or mechanical means, including information storage and retrieval systems, without written permission from the author, except for the use of brief quotations in a book review.

This book is a work of fiction. The story, all names, characters, and incidents portrayed in this production are fictitious. No identification with actual persons (living or deceased), places, buildings, and products is intended or should be inferred.

Cover: Best Page Forward

Editing: Sarah Pesce of Lopt & Cropt Editing

Proofread: Sandra Dee of One Love Editing

Description: Best Page Forward

ISBN: 979-8-88801-010-5 (ebook)

ISBN: 979-8-88801-011-2 (paperback)

ISBN: 979-8-88801-013-6 (audiobook)

Library of Congress Control Number: 2024914408

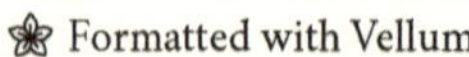 Formatted with Vellum

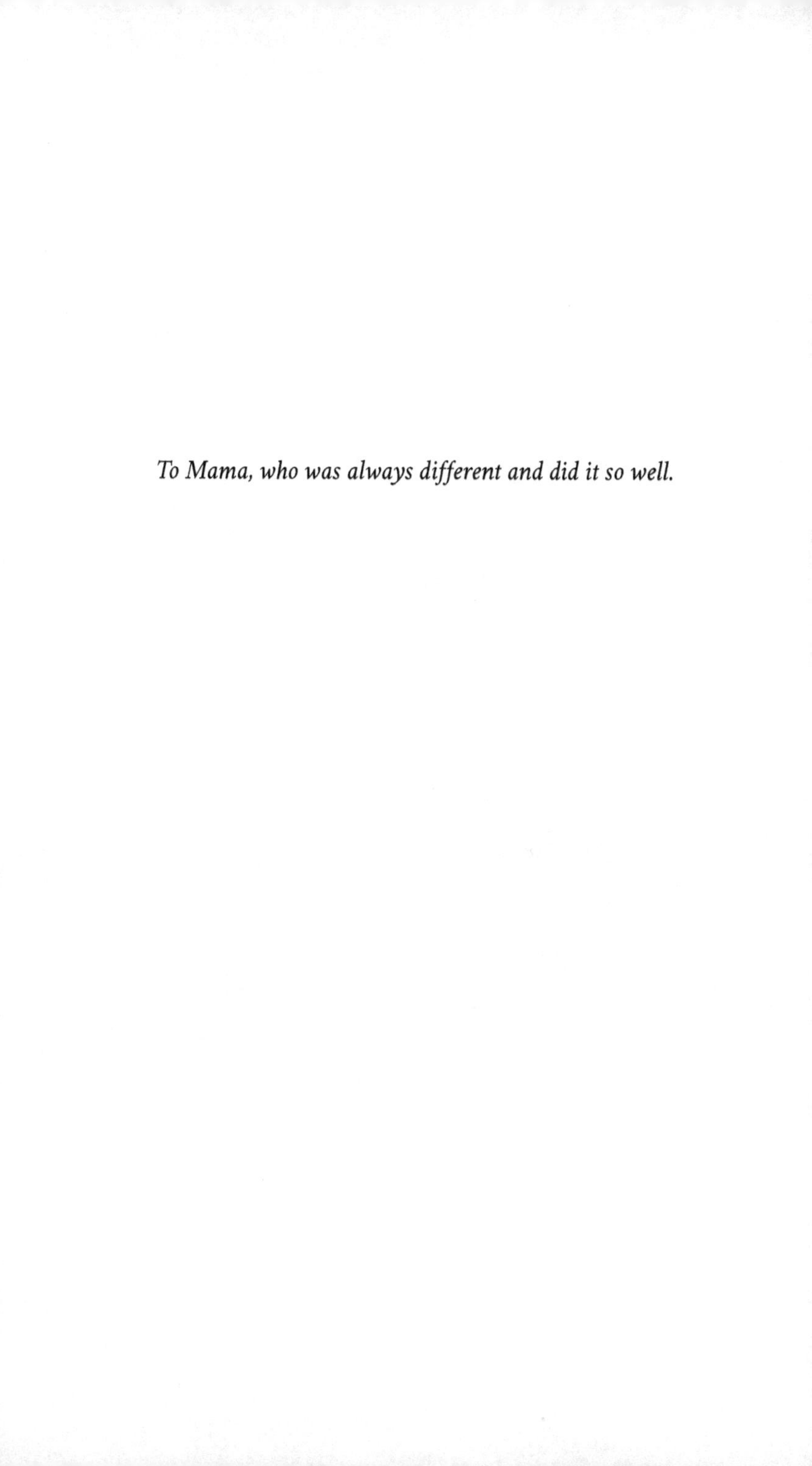

To Mama, who was always different and did it so well.

CHAPTER ONE

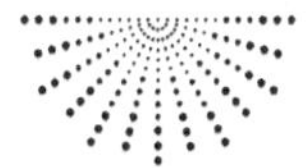

GRACE

Thirty seconds.

That's how long it took from flicking on the neon pink *Open* sign to her first customer walking in.

Around here, a cup of coffee was something to do.

Grace Hart let out a yawn as she plated cherry danishes, trying to get ahead of the morning rush. Not that she needed to worry about presentation. She could toss them into the pastry case like Frisbees, and they would still sell out by ten in the morning. Grace had her share of problems, but staying in business wasn't one of them. She hadn't had a slow day since opening up more than a year ago.

The bell chimed over the door to the Driftwood Coffee Company, and Grace closed the pastry case, wiping her hands on her apron. The icing left a smear on the pink fabric. But what did it matter? It wasn't like she had anyone to impress, and no one in Darling cared much about looks anyway. When a person had to get up at four in the morning, not having to look picture-perfect was a good thing.

The man standing at the counter fit the Alaskan stereotype to a T, taller than anyone she had ever met before, with shoulders that barely fit through the doorway and a big bushy beard.

She reached for a mug. "The usual?"

Mac Carter nodded and bent down to pet Ruby, Grace's mini Australian shepherd and her only serious relationship these days. At almost forty years old, Grace could confidently say it was her best relationship ever. She couldn't imagine living any other way.

Grace set up the filter for the pour-over, adding heaping scoops of freshly ground coffee. When she had first opened up for business, Mac's appearances in the shop had been sporadic. Now, he was her first customer every morning like clockwork.

He grabbed a bag of coffee beans from the display shelf that ran along the outside of the counter. "Can I get this ground?"

"Happy to." She traded the piping hot pour-over for the beans and Mac's dirty mug. The ceramic mugs were less wasteful than paper cups, though she still had those on hand for the occasional need. Most of the time, the locals remembered to trade in their dirty mugs for clean ones. The whole setup ran on an honor system that, while not perfect, was good enough. She couldn't ask for more than that.

Grace set the dirty mug in the dish bin before dumping the bag of coffee beans into the grinder. She didn't need to ask to know it was for Mac's wife, Elle.

If Mac was a walking Alaskan stereotype, then Elle was the exact opposite. The graceful blonde could get along with anyone and was a well-known lifestyle influencer. Meanwhile, Mac was a man of few words with a temper that could make up the difference. But after only a year, no one in town could now imagine a time when the two of them weren't together, Grace included. That's how love should be.

Grace used to think she and her ex-husband, Hunter, were like that. True love. Opposites attract. All the clichés. That was before she realized it wasn't a match made in heaven but rather its southern counterpart.

The worst part was that Hunter hadn't been the problem. She had. Hunter had shown her who he was from day one. It was Grace who had wanted something else, and after years of waiting, she had finally realized that Hunter would never be able to give it to her. So she had given it to herself. For better or for worse, having what she wanted meant a life without Hunter in it.

Grace fixed a smile on her face as she rang up the purchase and passed Mac the bag of ground coffee. It was far too early in the morning to be melancholy. The past was best left in the past.

Mac eyed the bookshelf longingly, both hands full.

Grace bit back a laugh. Mac was rarely in a joking mood, and she wasn't about to poke the bear before he'd had his first sip of morning coffee. "Don't tell me it's time for something new already. You've read them all by now."

Mac grunted, which could have conceivably been good-bye, and pushed the door open with his shoulder.

The *Borrow Me* sign swung as the door closed with a thump.

Just looking at the full bookshelves made Grace feel all warm and fuzzy inside. Her collection was enormous, hundreds of books in every genre. The romance novels were her favorites, and she wasn't embarrassed to admit it. Those stories had it all. Love. Adventure. Struggle. And no matter how bad things got, there was always a tidy happy ending. It was so much better than real life.

Grace never had a home to keep so many books before she moved to Alaska. As soon as she had a place of her own, she collected them like a woman possessed, filling every inch of space in the small apartment over her business. She eventually had to add shelves to the coffee shop to accommodate them.

Mac was the first to ask to borrow one. The rest was history. She suddenly had a coffee shop and an unofficial lending library. Like the mugs, it worked on an honor system, more or less. Again, there was a low bar for entertainment around here.

She hadn't dreamed of owning and operating a coffee shop on a small island in the middle of nowhere. But with a fifteen-year gap in her résumé and nothing but barista experience to support herself, it was the best idea she had been able to come up with at the time.

As far as living on an island in the middle of nowhere? It wasn't everyone's cup of coffee, but it had been exactly what Grace needed.

Space from Hunter.

Walking away from him had been the hardest thing she had ever done. She'd had no boundaries when it came to her ex-husband, and without space, Grace worried her resolve would melt away like sugar in hot espresso.

Except space wasn't exactly easy to achieve, considering that his work took him all over the world. But in all the years they had traveled together, he and Grace had never once set foot in Darling, and there certainly wasn't a reason for Hunter to do so now. The small Alaskan town wasn't exactly on the radar in the world of lifestyle photography, where Hunter had built his career.

Stifling another yawn, Grace fixed herself an Americano, knowing Mac had kicked off the parade of people who would come in between five in the morning and two in the afternoon when the coffee shop closed for the day. Driftwood was one of only two places in town to get a cup of coffee, and she definitely had the monopoly on danishes.

The espresso machine hummed as she pulled a shot before adding hot water to the mug. She was sure that if she kept the place open seven days a week, she would have business every single day. But Grace had struggled with setting boundaries before and refused to repeat history. She kept Sundays for herself.

Grace had just broken off the end of a freshly warmed croissant when the door swung open again. Taking a deep breath, she set aside her plate and stood behind the espresso machine.

The morning sped by with Grace making endless lattes, hot chocolates, and cappuccinos. The danishes were gone within a few hours, as predicted, quickly followed by the croissants and doughnuts.

This was her life now, and Grace liked it this way. No surprises, her days measured in shots of espresso and jumbo chocolate chip cookies. Some people might call it boring. But at least boring was safe.

Hunter could have the travel, the adventure, the glamor of her old life. He could have the whole world. But this corner of the Earth was hers.

* * *

IGNORING the ache in her shoulders, Grace wiped down the counters and twisted the rag over the sink. She was almost done cleaning up for the day when Ruby sat down in front of her and let out a yip.

Grace sighed. Even the dog knew the routine.

She grabbed a jacket before clipping on Ruby's leash. "I know, girl. You need to go out."

They walked around the back of the coffee shop, heading down towards the water. A bald eagle stared at them from a treetop while Ruby stuck a tentative paw in the frigid ocean.

The rocky shore was the complete opposite of the countless white-sand beaches Grace had traveled to during her marriage. In between lifestyle photoshoots, Hunter always wanted to squeeze in nature photography. It didn't pay the bills, but it was his true passion.

For more than a decade, they could never rest, never sit still. They were at home nowhere, and it had worn away at her the way the ocean pounded against rock until it slowly but surely disappeared. Towards the end of their marriage, it seemed almost nothing of Grace was left either. Not that Hunter had noticed.

Squinting against the glare of the overcast late-April day, Grace checked to make sure they were alone before letting Ruby off the leash. The fluffy dog ran down to the water, lunging at it with a bark and then running away when a wave broke.

Grace took a deep breath, refreshed by the crisp, salty air. Sometimes she had to pinch herself. After dreaming for so long of a place to call her own, she was finally home.

Who needed a hero? Grace had rescued herself.

Once her fingers and toes had turned cold, she clapped her hands and brought Ruby back to her. "Come on, girl. Let's go get something for dinner."

Walking back towards town, they made their way to the grocery store. Almost no one was out at this time of day. Darling didn't get busy until around dinnertime, when people would head to the Buck for hot food and cold beer. By then, Grace would be cozy in her apartment over the coffee shop. She wasn't one for going out these days. After all those years of being constantly on the go, she was more than happy to live a quiet life.

Grace knelt in front of the store, looping Ruby's leash around a post. "I'll be right back."

She pushed open the door, surprised to find she wasn't the only one out. "Hey, Charlotte. Nice to see you."

The older woman smiled and shifted her grocery bag to her other hip. "Hello, Grace. I was just grabbing a few things before the dinner rush. What are you up to?"

Grace lifted a shoulder. "Trying to figure out what the heck I'm going to eat tonight."

"It's hard to think of something when we make food all day for work, isn't it?" Charlotte sighed. "Why don't you come down to the Buck and get dinner there?"

Grace gave her a tight smile. Everyone in Darling was always nice to her. But being around people was the last thing she wanted to do after a long day at the coffee shop— or any day, really. She needed her space, to keep a protective bubble around herself, so she didn't get lost again. "Maybe another night. I'm not sure I feel up to it today."

"I can only imagine. I don't know how you run that place all by yourself. The Buck is enough for me with Wolfie—" Charlotte glanced at the door. "Speaking of, I better be getting back. See you sooner rather than later, I hope."

Grace lifted her hand to wave goodbye and started her own shopping. What Charlotte said didn't bother her. Not really. Grace enjoyed doing things by herself, tired or not.

What she didn't like was that it was so hard for other people to understand that. She had been on her own for two years now and in Darling for more than half of that time. What else would it take for people to accept this was how she wanted to live?

Her stomach growled and reminded her to focus. Grace selected a jar of spaghetti sauce, a package of pasta, and a loaf of sourdough bread.

She bit her lip as she paused in front of the shelves. Oh, what the heck? She grabbed a bottle of wine.

Grace piled her items on the counter and dinged the bell.

Vivian poked her head out of the back of the store. "You ready?"

"Yep. Dinner for one." Grace hoisted the wine overhead. "In case I forgot, Charlotte told me how impressive it is that I run the coffee shop on my own."

Vivian rolled her eyes as she walked over to the counter. She punched the prices into the ancient cash register. "I'm sure she was just trying to be nice. Trust me, I've heard it all. It seems people around here spend half the time assuring me I won't be alone forever and the other half feeling bad they said anything at all."

Grace nodded. She knew Vivian understood. When Grace had first moved to town, the young woman had barely spoken two words to her. But Vivian's family owned the grocery store that shared a wall with the cafe, so Grace saw her often.

It turned out Vivian was an incredible baker, and the mouthwatering pastry case at the Driftwood Coffee Company was all thanks to her. Over time, Grace had realized Vivian wasn't shy at all, just guarded. They had more than a shared wall in common.

More importantly, Vivian respected Grace's space, and Grace returned the favor. Probably another reason they got along so well, despite the decade age difference between the two of them. "Well, they don't need to feel bad. I don't feel bad about being single. In fact, I love it."

Vivian looked up from the cash register. "Speaking of, have you given any more thought to *it*?"

It. The dreaded dating app.

Grace shuddered. "I think my main takeaway from that

evening was never to drink more than two glasses of wine. That always seems to be the cause of my worst ideas."

Vivian laughed. "Don't you remember your speech? The whole thing about your fortieth birthday?"

Grace's shoulders sagged. She remembered alright. The problem was that she wanted to forget. "Can't we just ignore it? That's what adults do with their feelings."

"No way." Vivian shook her head, her stick-straight hair swaying. "You're doing this. I'm not letting you regret it. You'd do the same for me."

Grace gathered up her groceries, eager to get home and open the bottle of wine. Except this time, she wouldn't have a single drop over two glasses. "Does that mean you're getting on the dating app with me?"

Vivian smirked. "Are you kidding? *My* fortieth birthday is years away. You're on your own."

Precisely. Grace liked being on her own. What was so wrong with that?

* * *

IF GRACE WAS BEING COMPLETELY honest with herself, which was something she avoided as much as possible, there were a few things wrong with being on her own.

For one, she couldn't get the stupid spaghetti sauce open. After working up a sweat trying to twist off the lid, she finally poked around on the internet to find a solution. Grace tried the first suggestion and put a rubber band around the lid and the jar. It opened with a satisfying pop.

Ha! Problem solved. No man needed.

Then, the pasta somehow magically multiplied into enough to feed two people for a night or a single person for a week.

Grace shrugged it off. No worries. She could eat spaghetti seven days in a row.

But the third problem was slightly less solvable. It didn't rear its ugly head until the wine was open and half-gone.

The third problem was the truth.

If forced to admit it, she didn't always, totally, completely love being single.

Not that she missed Hunter at all. Going their separate ways had been the right decision. But maybe, if she met a different guy, the right guy, things could be better.

Grace didn't want to get married again, that was for sure. She liked her newfound independence. But dating would be a way to prove she was over Hunter once and for all. What could be a more perfect fortieth birthday present to herself than closure?

Besides, it wouldn't be awful to have someone to talk to or share a bottle of wine with. Or at least help her eat all this spaghetti.

Grace sighed. Why did Vivian have to bring up the whole stupid thing again? And to throw in that comment about being almost forty. Did the woman have no mercy?

But there was no avoiding it. Time would march on. Grace had figured that out the day she had woken up after fifteen years of marriage and realized that not only was she not happy, but she hadn't been for a very long time.

Grace reached for her book to distract herself. Who needed a guy when she had romances to read? No one in real life could compare to the heroes in her books. They always said the right thing, did the right thing, and gave her all the right feels. And at the end of the day, she could put the book down and walk away with no regrets.

But the western romance and its rough-around-the-edges cowboy hero failed to pull her in this time. Her eyes kept wandering to her phone, singing its siren call.

The possibility of something more than just words on a page.

The truth was that she hadn't needed Vivian to remind her. Grace remembered that night with annoying clarity, despite her best attempts to drown it in wine. She had even downloaded the dating app when she got back home. But she hadn't made a profile yet.

Grace went to the kitchen to refill her wineglass, bringing the bottle back with her.

Heart pounding, she grabbed her phone and tapped on the dating app icon.

Grace began building her account. She found one photo of herself she didn't totally hate. Hobbies and occupation were easy.

Distance? She cast the widest net. This was Alaska, after all.

What was she looking for? Not marriage. Never again. Grace had learned the hard way that the age-old institution wasn't for her.

Relationship status? With a curse word, she poured herself another splash of wine.

Now, that was the question of the century. She'd been trying to sort that out with her ex for the past two years. But the only thing he took seriously was his work. It had been that way their entire marriage.

Grace had sent emails and texts and had even called multiple times. Hunter always had some excuse. So finally, she gave up. What was the difference, anyway? They were already living separate lives for all intents and purposes.

But she was almost forty. The age when someone should at least know her own relationship status.

Ruby whined from her dog bed, lowering her head.

Grace scrolled through her contacts, tapping on The Big Mistake. "I know, girl. It's a terrible idea."

Ring. Ring. Ring.

Straight to voicemail. She scoffed. Shocker.

With another gulp of wine, Grace told her ex exactly what she thought of him.

Ending the call, she reached for the bottle, tipping it over her glass.

She frowned. Empty?

Now, that couldn't be good.

CHAPTER TWO

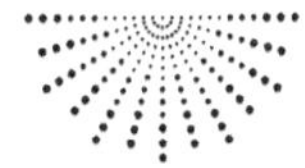

HUNTER

Thirty seconds.

That's how long it had taken his best friend to die.

It seemed life wasn't done kicking the shit out of Hunter Hart.

This trip was supposed to be a vacation. Lying on the beach. Plenty of ice-cold drinks. Hanging out with Jack.

Sometimes Hunter had to pinch himself. This couldn't possibly be his life. People didn't make careers out of traveling the world and taking pictures. But he had.

He couldn't believe his ex had given all this up. Before he could stop it, his brain reminded Hunter that she had given him up too.

A chill came over him, despite the warm late-spring day. He immediately tried to shake it off. That was her fault. She'd known what kind of person Hunter was when she married him. He wanted adventure. Grace was the one who had changed. Not him.

He tipped his head back, soaking up the sunshine. He

refused to let bad memories ruin his vacation. Hunter needed this trip. It seemed every month, his schedule was filled with more soul-sucking assignments than the month before. Assignments that, ironically, Grace would've loved.

Celebrity engagements. Haute couture fashion shows. Ad campaigns. The kind of assignments where someone could live a normal life with a permanent address.

"I know you love the nature stuff, but you can't climb mountains forever," his manager, Dana, had told him. "One day, you're going to get tired of folding yourself into little planes and holding a position for hours to get the perfect shot. You're going to want to be close to home. I'm trying to think of the long-term plan here. God knows you won't."

That had made Hunter laugh. He had a bank account that would make most people jealous. Last time he had checked, he had millions of followers on social media too. Though he had never been one for posting online regularly, so Dana had hired someone to manage that for him.

What he was doing was working. Long-term plan? This *was* the long-term plan.

But Hunter had one rule: never say no. It had led him into strange places, scary places, and boring places, but in the end, that rule had gotten him where he was. He didn't say no to learning photography in the first place or to his first assignment. If he had, he would be right back in Nevada, wondering when his life was going to start.

So he took the soul-sucking assignments, and he made them work. The secret was to never think about tomorrow, only today. It was the way he had always lived his life. And it had saved his sanity when his marriage ended.

"Hello, Earth to Hunter." Jack waved a hand in front of his face. "Everything okay?"

"Better than okay." Hunter dipped his chin.

He felt like he was floating. The late-April weather was

mild, but it seemed warmer, given the lack of a breeze. They had been drinking all day. Hunter hadn't eaten since dinner last night, and the alcohol had hit his bloodstream with the accuracy of a sniper.

A giggle grabbed his attention as a group of women walked by. Hunter and Jack had chartered a boat out to the gorgeous white-sand islands, but even in shoulder season, they weren't the only ones enjoying the perfect weather along the eastern Australian coast.

Jack sighed. "If this isn't heaven, I don't want to go."

His eyes were hidden behind sunglasses, but Hunter would bet money Jack was following the beach bunnies. Unlike Hunter, Jack had been smart enough to never get in a serious relationship.

Jack turned to him. "How are you doing?"

Hunter forced a smile and hoped it looked believable. "I'm doing great, man. You?"

Jack shook his head. "Your aunt—"

"We knew it was coming," Hunter interrupted, but not before the familiar nauseous feeling in his stomach came back. "She was older. Her health had been going downhill for more than a year. It's better this way. Better than her living in pain."

His friend took off his sunglasses, squinting into the bright sun as he looked at Hunter. "You're still allowed to be sad. You're allowed to have feelings."

Hunter's throat tightened. Jack was right. But Hunter had used logic to talk himself out of losing his mind when he had to say goodbye to the last relative he had a connection with. As if it wasn't enough to grow up without parents.

If he didn't keep moving, keep taking pictures, keep himself distracted, life would catch up with him. Hunter didn't know what else it would take from him, and he didn't want to find out. All he had left was work, and work kept Hunter alive.

In a cruel twist of fate, work also fueled his guilt, an unwelcome piece of baggage that Hunter had managed to drag all over the world despite his best intentions. All those years of going with the flow had resulted in a dream job. But his personal life was a nightmare. Every assignment he had taken also meant time not spent with the people he cared about, including his aunt. Now there wasn't any time left.

It was exactly why he was going to follow in Jack's footsteps and never relinquish his single status again. Then Hunter wouldn't have to choose between work and someone he loved. Because based on his track record, he had always chosen wrong. The last thing he needed was one more thing weighing on his soul, which was too damn heavy already.

"Have you talked to, you know, *her* at all?" Jack asked. "I'm sure she'd want to know."

Hunter looked away. Grace was another topic he preferred to avoid. She was the first person he'd thought of when his aunt had passed. He remembered holding the phone, his finger hovering over her name on the screen.

If anyone in the world would understand, it was Grace. She had always cared more about others than herself, even though she thought caring too much made her weak. To Hunter, it was her superpower.

But in the end, he hadn't called. Grace had made it clear. They lived separate lives now. They wanted different things. If he still had feelings for her, well, then he was an idiot.

"Nope. I should've never talked to her when I first saw her seventeen years ago. Look how well that worked out." Hunter finished his beer, washing away the memory of Grace smiling at him as they said their wedding vows. Towards the end of their relationship, he hadn't seen that smile much. "How about you? Looking forward to the next tour?"

Jack cracked his knuckles. "God, I wish. I swear, these kids get younger and younger. I'm practically geriatric next to them."

Hunter laughed. "You're one of the best golfers in the world. Next time I see you, you'll be telling me how you wiped the floor with them."

"Maybe." Jack's frown lines deepened. "Sometimes I wish I had done things differently. Don't you ever wonder what you're going to do when this is all over? And who you're going to do it with?"

"Nope. Trust me, dude. You did it right. Take it from a man who tried the marriage thing."

"Oh, yeah? I find that hard to believe. Take it from a man who knows you well enough to know you haven't been the same since you and Grace split. You two had something real."

Hunter's chest grew tight, and he glanced away. Maybe they did. But whatever it was had run its course. He stood from his beach towel. "I'm going to go cool off."

Jack followed him, mercifully understanding that the topic of Grace was closed. What was left to say when Hunter wasn't even sure what the hell had happened? The only person who could help him understand was Grace herself. Too bad she couldn't stand him these days.

Leaving their drinks and towels behind, Hunter and Jack waded into the shallow waves lapping against the sugar shore.

Hunter's shirt stuck to his back with sweat. The turquoise water felt like an angel's kiss against his legs. "God, that feels good."

"Ow!" Jack cried out. He bent over, reaching into the water. "Holy crap. Look how huge this thing is!"

Jack held up the cone shell, grinning.

What happened next was so fast Hunter wasn't sure what he saw until it was over.

Whatever was in the shell reached out, sticking Jack in the neck. Within seconds, his body crumpled in the water, the ocean washing over the top of his head with a crash.

Hunter pulled Jack out of the water, shaking his friend, slapping his face, begging him to wake up.

But Jack was dead before he hit the ground.

The few other people on the beach ran over, gathering around Hunter and Jack. They tried to talk to Hunter, and someone touched his arm. But their voices were nothing but background noise.

Hunter had a moment of clarity, thinking back to just a little while ago when he had thought that he had lost everyone he had loved.

Now, he truly had.

* * *

THE FIRST PERSON he called was Dana. It was the middle of the night where she was, but she still answered. She always did. Dana was the closest thing he had left to family. The only one he had left at all, really. "I'll take care of everything. Whatever you need."

"The body—" Hunter's voice cracked. He covered his eyes as hot tears rolled down his face.

Dana wasn't fazed. She spoke slowly in a calm tone, as if he was crazy. Maybe he was. He couldn't make sense of anything. "I told you, I'll figure it out. I'll get in touch with his manager. Your job is to get home and take care of yourself. It was a freak accident, okay? You didn't do anything wrong."

Just watched his friend die in front of him, helpless to do anything.

For the first time in his life, Hunter canceled an assignment. Did it even matter? Did anything?

When Dana had emailed him the details for his flight home, Hunter had to stare at it for a minute, his address strange to his own eyes. The one-bedroom apartment was more of a storage than a home. He was only ever there for a weekend at a time, and sometimes not for months.

He didn't need the place, not really. But the sad truth was it was one of the last connections he had with Grace. They had met in Las Vegas, and he couldn't quite bring himself to let go of this apartment, even though holding on to it was pointless.

Hunter blinked his eyes open. Was it morning? Night? Hard to tell with the curtains always closed. Hard to tell when the only time he got up was to drink himself back into oblivion.

Dana called him once a day to make sure he was still alive. He told her she didn't need to bother. So she started calling him twice a day.

He meant it, though. She didn't need to worry. The only thing that would make Hunter feel more guilty about Jack would be ending his own life on purpose when Jack hadn't had the choice.

Hunter's social media manager handled his accounts. Dana handled his calendar. Jack's family handled the funeral.

If only someone could handle his life for him. If only he didn't have to think. Because he was losing it.

Hunter couldn't trust himself. If he went to sleep, he saw Jack fall to the ground over and over again. And when Hunter was awake, he played a more conscious role in torturing himself.

Dana was right. It was a freak accident. Something he could've never seen coming.

Something that might've never happened if Hunter hadn't

suggested going into the water to get away from the conversation about Grace.

Grace, the only person Hunter wanted to talk to. If only she didn't hate his guts.

He and his wife had parted on no uncertain terms. She had told him exactly where to go, and it wasn't heaven. It could've been worse. She could've made all kinds of demands, demands that would've held up in a court of law. But all she asked was to be left alone.

His phone vibrated again, bouncing around the nightstand. Hunter swept it into the drawer, making it disappear with a satisfying slam. The world could wait. It had been a week, but he still wasn't ready to face real life.

Wandering into the kitchen, Hunter grabbed a fresh bottle of whiskey, cracking the cap. He didn't bother with a glass.

He knew it wasn't helping, staying holed up in his apartment with just himself and his thoughts and booze. But there was nowhere he wanted to go.

Hunter sat on the couch and took sips of the liquor until he felt the room spin. Setting it on the table, he tripped his way back into the bedroom.

A muted beep came from the drawer.

He clenched his jaw. That's it. He was going to turn the damn thing off. Dana knew where he lived if she really needed to talk to him. Everyone else could wait forever as far as he cared.

Voicemail blinked at him from the screen. Hunter didn't recognize the area code. He was a curious cat, or however the phrase went. He frowned. The whiskey made it hard to remember.

"Hunter. It's Grace. Remember me? Look, it's time. We need to finish the paperwork. I'm about to turn forty. Forty!

Screw you. This stupid dating app wants to know my relationship status? Well, you tell me."

When Hunter would listen to that voicemail two days later, he would hear the anger in her voice. He would notice the hiccup, wonder if perhaps Grace wasn't exactly stone-cold sober when she called.

But all he focused on at that moment was the fact that she had called.

Hunter rubbed his forehead as he tried to remember where she was. Charming? Sweetheart? No, Darling. Darling, Alaska.

Ridiculous name.

With one eye closed to help him focus, he tapped on the phone screen and pulled up Darling on the map.

Oh hell. Truly the middle of nowhere.

He straightened. Where better to go than nowhere when he didn't want to be anywhere?

Dragging his sorry ass from bed, Hunter stumbled into the shower.

He had a plane to catch.

CHAPTER THREE

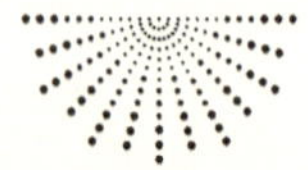

GRACE

Grace groaned and shoved her phone into her apron pocket. "In case you were wondering, dating apps suck."

"That bad, huh?" Vivian asked.

"The worst. The closest guy who looks kind of okay is almost five hours away."

Vivian laughed. "That's not a dating app problem. That's an Alaska problem."

Grace tidied up the sugar packets. It was already the first week of May, and her birthday was less than a month away. She wasn't going to meet someone between now and then. Maybe closure would be next year's present to herself if she got the wild hair to try this again. "Yeah, well, it's not my problem anymore. I'm going to give up."

"What? No, you can't! It's only been a week! You're supposed to be a good example for me."

Grace narrowed her eyes. "Is that a comment about my age?"

"No, ma'am. But really. You were married before. How did you meet your husband?"

Grace chewed on her lip. She almost never talked about her life before Darling. She didn't just need physical space from Hunter. She needed space from the memories too.

For the last two years, when Grace thought about Hunter, her shoulders would climb to her ears. To say he left her with a bad taste was an understatement.

But the Hunter that she had first met? The guy she had fallen in love with seventeen years ago? She hadn't thought about him in a long time. He had even given her romance book heroes a run for their money.

"I was working at a coffee shop that featured local artists. He walked in one day to ask about putting his photos up, and… never mind. It sounds so cheesy."

"Tell me," Vivian begged.

"God, it's so cliché." Grace shook her head. "But it really was love at first sight. He had long red hair and gray eyes and a dimple that just melted my heart."

"He sounds dreamy."

Grace's stomach turned ooey-gooey at the memory of how the rest of the world faded away the first time she saw Hunter. "He was."

Probably still is. It would be easy to look up his social media accounts and find out. But that didn't exactly align with giving up Hunter cold turkey, so Grace didn't tempt fate.

"See?" Vivian smiled. "That's why you can't give up. Not yet. You never know."

Grace threw her arms in the air. "You've lived in Darling your whole life. You know better than I do that a hot single guy is not going to randomly walk in here one day."

The door opened just then, the daylight highlighting a tall form.

Grace sucked in her breath. Shadow obscured his face. But she would've recognized him anywhere.

"Hello, Grace."

Her stomach dropped through the floor. "What the hell are you doing here?"

"Come on, sweetheart. Is that any way to talk to your husband? Or did you forget we're still married?"

* * *

No way.

There was no way that Hunter Hart was standing in front of her right now.

His red hair was cut shorter than it had been the day they had first met. He'd changed the style after his photography career had taken off. Same gorgeous gray eyes, though.

She'd bet the dimple hadn't disappeared. But Hunter wasn't smiling.

Grace let out a short laugh, even though she felt more like screaming and running into the forest, never to look back. "Forget? Are you kidding? I sleep with the divorce papers under my pillow, hoping that the tooth fairy might help me out. Lord knows it would take a miracle to get them signed."

He shifted to his other foot. Even with dark circles under his eyes, standing there in a wrinkled T-shirt, he was still the hottest guy she'd ever seen. It only added to her irritation. "I meant to get around to it. Sorry."

Her face grew warm as she remembered all the reasons why it hadn't worked out between them. Apparently, Hunter still never thought much past tomorrow. Living in the moment was a way of life for him, regardless of how it affected other people.

"A half-assed apology doesn't mean you can just barge in

here. Just sign the damn papers already so we can be unmarried. It's been two years, for Christ's sake."

He shrugged. "Lost them."

Grace saw red. Leave it to Hunter to act nonchalant about this. He never took anything but his photography seriously. Not her. Not their relationship. "Then I'll get new ones from the attorney."

Vivian stepped away. "I think I'll head back to the store."

Grace looked at her friend. She had forgotten Vivian was even there. "Don't feel like you have to go."

Vivian gave her a look that said she would rather be anywhere but here. Grace didn't blame her. Talking about her past was bad enough. A live re-enactment was even worse. "See you later."

As Vivian walked out of the coffee shop, Grace stood as tall as she could, stretching to all of her five feet, nine inches. This was her territory, and she'd be damned if she let Hunter walk all over her. "I hope you have a good reason for being here. And a return flight scheduled."

She braced herself for Hunter to push back. She wouldn't give in as easily as she had time and time again back when they were married. But instead, the pain she saw in his eyes almost knocked her over. "I need to be here, Grace."

"Hunter. What the hell happened?"

His Adam's apple bobbed. "A lot."

"You can't tell me?"

He dropped his gaze to the floor. "It's Jack."

"Jack? What happened with Jack?"

"He's dead." Hunter's voice cracked.

Grace's throat grew tight. Jack had been a good guy, and she knew how much he'd meant to Hunter. Against her will, she felt sympathy for the man falling to pieces in front of her. She had come to think of him as the villain over the past few years. But he was a person, too. Someone she used to love.

Not anymore, her brain reminded her.

"Hunter, I'm so sorry. What happened?"

He shook his head. "I can't even think about it right now."

Grace understood the feeling. She knew better than to press on his bruises.

But Hunter was here in her coffee shop, her corner of the world. She had fought for this place, this life. It had taken every ounce of strength she had. And she wouldn't give it up just because she felt bad for the guy. Grace had compromised too much for Hunter over the years already, and she refused to do it one more time. "I understand that you're grieving. But I don't understand how you ended up here, of all places."

He let out a laugh, a raw sound that was anything but happy. It scraped against her heart. He was in bad shape. "I don't know how either. Just needed to get away, I guess."

"And your estranged wife was the best option?"

Hunter looked her in the eye. "You've always been the most important person in my life, Grace. Where else would I go?"

The inner peace she had built up over the past two years disappeared like a sandcastle beneath ocean waves.

No one could undo her like Hunter Hart.

CHAPTER FOUR

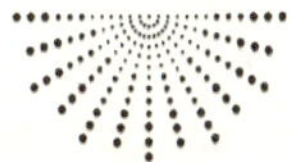

HUNTER

What was that saying? Time heals all wounds? Yeah, well, time had done nothing for how he felt about Grace.

He wanted to hate her. He wanted to look at her and feel nothing at all. Anything besides wishing he could rewind time so that he could live all those years together again.

Why did Grace still have to be so damn gorgeous? She was standing behind the espresso machine, looking like a dream, just like the day they met. Though she had probably repressed that memory by now.

Except unlike that day, she was asking questions he didn't know the answers to. Hunter wanted to tell her the truth. He did. But it didn't make sense to him either.

Jack had to be looking down at Hunter and laughing right now. Jack always told him letting Grace walk away was the stupidest thing Hunter had ever done. Maybe his friend was right. Look where Hunter was standing, after all.

"I know you're not my biggest fan."

Grace crossed her arms. "That's an understatement."

He took a shaky breath. How Grace felt about him wasn't a surprise. The surprise was how much it still hurt. "I came all this way. You can't cut me any slack? Does fifteen years of marriage count for nothing?"

"If only you knew how often I asked myself that same question."

Hunter swallowed. He had tried to talk to Grace when she had left. He had begged her to tell him what he could do to fix things between them. She had told him it wouldn't change a thing. Hunter still had no idea what exactly made her wake up one morning and decide to walk away from their life together. "What do you want me to do? Ride a polar bear back home?"

"There aren't polar bears here." Grace rolled her eyes. "There is a lodge in town. I'll see if they have any rooms. May is the beginning of tourist season, though, so don't be shocked if you end up with a cot in the laundry room."

"I forgot how much I missed domestic bliss," Hunter snapped. "Being married is such a joy."

Grace stuck her tongue at him and held her cell phone to her ear.

He pressed his lips together. His nerves were raw right now, and it only took the faintest touch to set him off. He didn't come here to argue. He hated fighting with Grace.

Hunter turned his back to her, and his eyebrows shot up his forehead. Jesus Christ, that was a lot of books. He didn't even own enough books to fill a single shelf. A person couldn't drag that much crap around the world.

So this was what Grace had wanted? Why she had left him? Hunter would never understand giving up the life they had, and definitely not for this tiny little town in Alaska.

This was a damn nightmare. Stuck in one spot? Buried beneath a pile of stuff? Every day the same? No, thanks.

Hunter could never do it. And luckily, he had created a life where he didn't have to.

Grace cursed, and Hunter turned to look at her. She slipped her phone back in her pocket. "They'll have an opening in three nights. If for some reason you haven't left town by then, the room has your name on it. For now, I guess you can stay here."

Her tone dared him to argue. Too bad for her. He was in the mood to stir up trouble. "Are you serious? I come here, to middle-of-nowhere Alaska, after my best friend died, and you're going to pass me off to some hotel?"

"Hunter," she said, her voice soft. For some reason, that unsteadied him more than her being annoyed. "I feel for you. I really do. If you want to talk about Jack, let's talk. But you staying here would be asking for trouble."

He clenched his jaw. Maybe trouble was what he wanted. Trouble would be a distraction from the pain.

"Besides." She gave him a half-smile. "Don't pretend you don't love being in the middle of nowhere."

Hunter stopped himself before he smiled back. Grace had done it again. She reached inside and stirred up all sorts of emotions, emotions he had become an expert at ignoring since he'd last seen her. "Maybe the lodge would be the best idea."

Look how mixed up he felt just from being in the same room as Grace for a few minutes. Who knew what kind of shape he'd be in after a few days together?

She raised an eyebrow. "Any chance I could get you to sign those divorce papers while I'm on a winning streak? Oh wait, you lost them. Or forgot. Whatever your excuse was."

Hunter stiffened. "Is there a reason you want to get rid of me so damn bad?"

"Besides the fact that we separated two years ago?" She glanced away. "The truth is, I want to date again."

Hunter sucked in his breath. It shouldn't feel like a punch to the stomach. They had been split up for a while, for Christ's sake. Hunter should be one hundred percent over this relationship.

Except the idea of Grace being with anyone else made him feel sick. It was almost as bad as the thought of him being with someone who wasn't Grace. "Dating again. Good social scene in Alaska?"

She made a face. "God no. The odds are good, but the goods are odd."

"So that means—"

"I've joined a dating app."

Hunter couldn't help it. It was the worst possible reaction. It made no sense. But he laughed.

And laughed.

And laughed.

Grace scowled at him. "Something funny?"

Hunter dragged a hand down his face. "You can't be serious."

"Why? You think I'm that much of a loser?"

"Oh, honey. It's not you I am worried about. It's those poor men. Not one of them will be good enough."

Hunter sure as hell hadn't been. And he had tried. Tried harder than he had at anything his whole life, even his photography career. In the end, he still wasn't sure what exactly had gone wrong between him and Grace.

But he was sure of one thing after ten minutes back in her presence. He still wasn't over her. At this rate, he might not ever be. He really was a glutton for punishment.

"God, I can't wait to meet someone normal," Grace muttered through gritted teeth. "And don't call me honey."

"You really want to date again?"

"Yes," she said, breaking his heart all over again.

Hunter picked up his bag. "Then it's a good thing I'm staying here."

She narrowed her eyes. "Why? What does you staying here have to do with my dating life?"

He held her gaze. "Because I know you, *honey*. And I want to be there when you realize normal isn't what you want at all."

CHAPTER FIVE

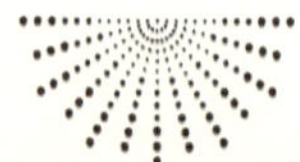

GRACE

Grace tried to ignore the shiver that ran down her back. Pure animal attraction. Nothing serious. Nothing real. Just because she hadn't been able to resist Hunter when they first met didn't mean history was repeating itself. She did not love him anymore, and that's what she had to remember. "What makes you think that you have any idea what I want?"

He made his way over to the staircase. "I'm assuming this is the way up?"

Grace pressed her lips together, fuming. Of course he ignored her question. He had only been here a few minutes, and already, he was back to his old tricks, living in the moment and doing what worked for him.

Before she could answer, tiny claws tapped against the wood floor as Ruby came down the staircase. She let out two quick barks at Hunter.

He glanced at Grace. "A dog."

"Thanks, Captain Obvious."

He stepped around Ruby. "No one says that anymore."

As he disappeared upstairs, Grace slapped the bell on the counter and took the stairs two at a time. She found Hunter poking his head in her bedroom.

"That's my room," she gasped, her lungs burning.

"Not much for cardio these days, are we?"

Grace shot him a look. She'd like to see him take the stairs two at a time. But as much as she hated to admit it, Hunter looked like he was still in great shape. That was her husband. He had always looked just as good in front of the camera as behind it.

"I guess this one is mine, then." Hunter stuck his bag inside the spare room next to hers. "Which way to the bathroom?"

She pointed down the hall, relieved to have a minute to herself to think. Hunter followed her directions, closing the door behind him.

Ruby whined and sat at Grace's feet.

"I know, girl," Grace whispered. "This is bad."

As soon as she went downstairs, Grace was going to find a lawyer. There wasn't one in Darling. She'd have to go to Ketchikan or maybe Juneau. But it would be worth it. Grace wasn't about to let Hunter run her life again without consulting with a professional.

She was still struggling to wrap her head around the fact that he was *here*. Never once had Grace imagined Hunter stepping through the door to the coffee shop. That was the whole point of living in the middle of nowhere.

She mentally kicked herself for not pushing harder for the divorce when they first separated. Grace had tired of Hunter's excuses, had tired of long emails and texts that he answered with just an emoji. She had spent more time talking to his voicemail than him.

And should she be surprised that he hadn't taken their

separation seriously? The only surprise would've been if he hadn't disappointed her.

Hunter came back from the bathroom. "This place is cute."

As if she gave a damn about his opinion of her home. What did he know anyway? Hunter didn't even want a home. "Where's your laptop?"

"Backpack like always. You know that. Why?"

"Because you're buying a plane ticket back right now."

He barked a laugh. "You're hilarious. I'm not going anywhere."

Grace took a deep breath. She reminded herself to have compassion. Hunter had just lost his best friend. But there were other places he could stay. "What about your aunt? I'm sure she'd love to see you. Hawaii is always nice. Very peaceful. Much better than Alaska."

He glanced away, and Grace swore his eyes glistened. Was he crying? "Aunt Linda passed away."

Her face fell. Shit. She was really striking out today. "When? Why didn't you tell me?"

"A couple of months ago. I wanted to tell you. But I didn't know how."

Grace's heart squeezed. She understood. There were still moments when the first person she wanted to talk to about her problems was Hunter. Until she remembered things were different now. That they had to be different, or it would be too easy to get lost in him again. "I'm so sorry, Hunter."

Two huge losses. No wonder the poor guy showed up at her door like a homing device. Maybe he really didn't want to be here. Maybe he just needed to be for a bit. "You know what? We can talk about your plan to get out of here another day."

So much for being a hard-ass. Sometimes she really hated herself.

"Thanks, Grace."

She held up a finger. "But we are going to have ground rules. Because I can't do this again."

"Do what?"

Grace gestured between them. "Us."

His eyes softened. "I don't remember it being all bad."

"No, don't do that. Don't be sweet."

Hunter lifted the corner of his mouth. "Is that one of the ground rules?"

Before she could answer, a sound came from downstairs. Grace cocked her head, uncertain if she heard the bell or just imagined it. Sometimes she heard the damn sound in her sleep.

The dinging continued.

"I think someone is here," Hunter said in a mock whisper.

She narrowed her eyes. "Don't you dare touch anything. And don't forget. Ground rules."

"It's a date!" he called out as she ran down the stairs.

Grace's shoulders pinched together. Three nights had never seemed so long.

Elle stood in front of the counter. "Hey, Grace, how's it going?"

"Interesting." Grace forced a smile. "How can I help you?"

"I wanted to get some coffee for my manager. Sending her a little birthday package. I almost asked Mac to grab something this morning, but I wanted to choose the blend myself."

Grace reached for the foil bag closest to her. Even though she usually enjoyed chatting with Elle, she needed to get back upstairs before Hunter got a little too comfortable. "How about this new medium roast? It has a hint of cardamom."

Elle wrinkled her nose. "I'm not against the cardamom, but that might be too exotic for her."

Grace poured a small cup, splashing a little on the

counter in her rush. "Here, I have some in the air pot. Let me know what you think."

As Elle accepted the sample, footsteps sounded on the stairs. She arched a blonde brow. "I didn't know you had company."

"I don't," Grace muttered.

Hunter rounded the corner, his dimple making an appearance as he smiled at Elle and reached out his hand. "Hunter Hart. Nice to meet you."

Grace's pulse fluttered, and she commanded her hormones to get a grip. That dimple was nothing but empty promises.

Elle gaped at him. "I know you. You're the photographer. Oh my God. Hart. I never put that together."

Grace's stomach knotted up. This was exactly why she didn't like to talk about her personal life before Darling. This was supposed to be her fresh start. New Grace had boundaries. New Grace wasn't a pathetic pushover. New Grace wasn't just a supporting character in Hunter's life. "There's nothing to put together. We aren't together. Elle, please meet my ex-husband."

"I'm a huge fan. Your photos are beautiful," she gushed as she shook Hunter's hand. "Elle Blessing. Nice to meet you."

His eyes lit up. "And I know you. My manager is a huge fan of yours. I can't believe Grace never told me you lived in town."

Grace bit back the urge to remind Hunter that she hadn't told him because they had barely talked in two years.

Elle looked back and forth between the two of them. "And I still can't believe you two are a thing."

Grace shook her head. "*Were* a thing."

Hunter lifted a shoulder, as if shocking revelations were daily occurrences for him. Of course, life didn't excite him anymore. He had done it all. "Can't make this stuff up."

Grace glared at him. "You can, however, mind your own business."

Elle cleared her throat. "You know what? Why don't I come back another time?"

"No, please," Grace said. "Let's get that coffee for your manager."

Elle held up the sample cup. "I'll take this one."

Whether Elle really wanted that blend or if she just wanted to get the hell out of the cafe, Grace rang up the purchase all the same.

Not that she could blame Elle for wanting to leave. A person could cut the tension with a knife. Although if Grace had a knife right now, she'd be tempted to give Hunter a little poke.

He really brought out the worst in her. Yet another reason they were better off living separate lives.

After Elle had left, Grace turned to Hunter. "Can you please stop scaring people away?"

His smile disappeared and the dimple along with it. "Can you please stop blaming me for everything?"

Grace clenched her fists as Hunter disappeared back upstairs. Oh, she blamed him alright. But he had no idea what she blamed him for. Even if he did, it wouldn't change things between them.

The bell over the door chimed, and she quickly composed herself. Grace was determined to get through the day without scaring away any more potential customers. If she was going to have a breakdown, it would have to wait until after she closed for the day.

Grace had one order after another, her stomach twisting tighter with each passing minute. At this rate, she wouldn't be able to finish her conversation with Hunter until she closed up. By then, he'd probably be moved in.

She shouldn't have let him through the front door. But he

had caught her off guard, showing up here with the weight of the world on his shoulders. The Hunter she knew let everything roll off his back like water off a duck.

Grace only had herself to blame. For all of her grand declarations, she was no better than Pavlov's dogs. Get her within ten feet of Hunter, and her resolve became flakier than the croissant she enjoyed for breakfast every morning. And now he was upstairs. In her home. In her space. How the hell had that even happened?

Old Grace would've held him. Done anything she could to make it better. She would've turned her life upside down if it meant making his world right. Old Grace had truly loved Hunter. Or at least she thought she did.

It had taken everything she had to walk away from him before. Maybe it would have been different if she'd had family or friends or a place to call home. But it was so easy to second-guess herself, to wonder if she was the crazy one, as they went around the world again and again and again.

She wanted to believe every promise Hunter had made to her. Maybe this would be the last year on the road, then they would have a home. Maybe after this assignment, then they would try for children. Nothing changed. Her dreams were constantly delayed, like a dentist appointment that kept getting rescheduled by a nervous patient.

The irony was that a million women would've gladly traded lives with her. A handsome and talented husband. A life of travel and adventure. A healthy bank account.

Grace welcomed anyone who wanted her life to have it. See how they liked always following Hunter around, always being the assistant. See how fulfilled they were helping someone else with his dreams and never living their own. See how they slept at night, wondering if they were their own person or an extension of their husband.

Sometimes Grace wished she had never met Hunter. She

could've kept working at the coffee shop, finished her business degree, and married someone normal. Lived a life that was normal.

I want to be there when you realize normal isn't what you want at all.

She bristled. Let Hunter think what he wanted. From where she stood, normal looked pretty good. Although if someone normal could have the same gray eyes and chiseled abs, she wouldn't complain. A dimple would be nice.

Damn that dimple.

Milk boiled over in the frothing tin, burning her hand. Grace cursed and grabbed a dish rag to clean up the mess. Already, he was undoing her, thread by thread.

She steeled her nerves. If Hunter thought she was the same woman he used to know, then he was in for a surprise. She would be stronger this time. Less forgiving. More selfish.

Grace spent the rest of the day reliving every bad memory, remembering every reason she finally told Hunter it was over and walked away from him.

She understood that he was grieving right now. But Grace would feel better once he had his return ticket. That was something they would discuss tonight, along with the ground rules.

Hunter showing up was a plot twist she hadn't seen coming. Grace had no idea what to expect next, and she didn't like the unknowns looming before her.

But Grace knew one thing for sure.

She would not, could not, fall back in love with Hunter Hart.

CHAPTER SIX

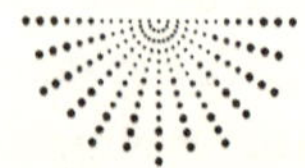

Can you please stop blaming me for everything?

Maybe he was to blame. But for what exactly? Loving her too much? Living a dream life? What was so wrong with that? From what Hunter could remember, it had been pretty good.

Nostalgia plucked on his heartstrings. It was impossible to be around Grace and not think of those first few adventures. The thrill of being paid for his work while they traveled to locations they could have never afforded themselves. It never got old to him. But both Hunter and the adventures had gotten old to Grace.

Shaking off the memories, Hunter poked around the apartment while Grace was in the coffee shop. The space was small for two people, but he could make it work. It wasn't like he stayed exclusively at five-star hotels. Some photoshoots took him to places where his only choice for accommodations was one step up from sleeping in the dirt. This was luxurious by comparison.

Hunter went back to the guest room to lie down for a bit, closing his eyes. Despite being exhausted, he couldn't sleep. He hadn't slept in days. Probably something else that had contributed to the cockamamy idea to show up on Grace's doorstep. Sleep deprivation never made for good decisions.

The problem was that he was terrified to sleep. Hunter didn't want to see Jack fall to the ground over and over again. In real life, it happened so quickly. But his nightmares tortured him, dragging out every second.

If only Jack hadn't picked up that seashell. If only they'd known about the deadly creature that lived inside it.

He couldn't cry anymore. It was a freak accident. His brain knew he wasn't to blame, but his heart wasn't listening.

Instead, his heart had an agenda of its own, whispering that Hunter had done it again. Lost someone he would never get back. Didn't spend enough time with someone when he had the chance. And all he had left was regret.

Whining came from the side of the bed, and Hunter reached down to find the miniature Australian shepherd. He buried his hand in the soft fur, and the dog licked his arm.

Hunter wasn't a fan of dogs. He didn't mind the smell or the dog hair. No, it was the responsibility that was the problem. How the hell was a guy with his lifestyle ever supposed to take care of a dog? But for some reason, he felt better right now than he had since before. Before everything changed. Before he had lost everyone he cared about.

Footsteps pounded on the staircase, and his back tensed. He knew Grace wanted answers. He wished he could explain what happened, exactly why he had to be here. All Hunter knew was that he couldn't do life right now. He needed her. Grace and her coffee shop in the middle of nowhere, cut off from the real world. Grace, who blamed him for everything.

"Ruby?" Grace's voice called out, followed by a whistle. "Here, girl."

The dog hopped to her feet, her nails clicking against the wood floor.

Grace popped her head inside the room. "You can just close the door if Ruby is bothering you."

"She's not bothering me."

Grace's face soured. "Well, you're bothering me. I called an attorney in Ketchikan. We're taking the ferry over tomorrow."

"Tomorrow?" Hunter sat up. "You sure don't waste any time."

"You've wasted more than enough for the both of us." She gave him a pointed look. "Couldn't have just signed the paperwork two years ago."

Hunter cracked his neck. He didn't want to let her get to him. Didn't want to completely fall apart, assuming he hadn't already. He had shown up at his estranged wife's home in remote Alaska, after all. The forecast for his sanity wasn't looking so good. "Whatever. I have nothing better to do."

Grace glanced around the room. "I wouldn't bother unpacking."

His shoulders pinched together. Hunter had always been the fun, well-liked guy. The guy who was a good time. How did he end up the villain in all this? "I'm not trying to be the bad guy here."

She let out a bitter laugh. "That's rich."

He winced. Would Grace ever stop hating him? Where was the woman he had married? The one who loved him as deeply as he had loved her? Grace wanted answers? So did Hunter, and there was no time like the present. "What the hell happened with us?"

"That's something I've asked myself a million times. I'm just stupid, I guess."

His heart squeezed. So it wasn't just Hunter that Grace didn't have compassion for these days. She didn't have any for herself, either. "You're not stupid. You're the smartest person I know."

Grace shook her head. "I am stupid. I was so in love with you that all I cared about was making you happy."

"I thought we were both happy."

"*You* were happy. Why wouldn't you have been? We chased *your* dreams. We lived *your* life. You had everything you wanted." She lifted her chin, and her dark eyes danced, daring him to challenge her. It killed him to have this wall between them.

"I'm sorry." It probably sounded as pathetic to her as it did to him. But he didn't know what else to say. Sorry seemed like a good place to start.

"The only thing I am sorry about is that I wasted so much time. I'll never be that desperate again." The steel edge of her voice told Hunter she was not someone to underestimate. But then again, she never had been.

She turned on her heel and left without another word.

Hunter flopped back on the bed and stared up at the ceiling. No one could stir him up like Grace.

That's why he'd come here, right? To be pulled back to life, kicking and screaming? Because after traveling the world, he realized there was no one else like her. But it was too late for that now. All she cared about was the divorce.

His stomach twisted. He hadn't lost the damn papers, of course. No, he had kept them in his backpack, tucked into his laptop sleeve. Those papers were more well traveled than almost anyone he knew. Hunter had told himself he had been busy, plain and simple.

Grace had hounded him at first, demanding Hunter do his part so they could move on with their lives. But over time, her emails and phone calls and texts were shorter and less frequent until they had dried up altogether. In a way, that had bothered him more than her being pissed off. It's like she had stopped caring about him completely.

Hunter hadn't known what the hell to do, so he'd done nothing. He was angry, hurt, and confused. He had thought she'd be back. Maybe she just needed some space after years of spending almost every moment together.

A day turned into a week. Then it was a month, a year, and then almost two. Surely she'd come around, right?

He had been wrong.

Maybe if Hunter had told her the truth, she would've had more patience with him. Because the fact of the matter was, Hunter had never been as brave as Grace.

Grace had asked him more than once about slowing down one of these days, having a place they could call their own, and eventually a family. Hunter had thought they would get around to it. But not yet. He wasn't ready to pump the brakes on his career.

People acted like Hunter had this great, God-given talent. But the truth was, work was the only thing he could do right. Hunter didn't know who he would be if he hadn't caught lightning in a bottle with his photography career. The thought terrified him.

Not Grace. She didn't leave Hunter for a career or another relationship. She left because their life wasn't working for her, and the possibility of a different life was enough to pull her away. The promise of something different had been all it had taken, and that had almost killed Hunter.

He had turned it over and over in his head. He had thought about it in Australia, in Scotland, in Brazil. Hunter had talked himself into believing they weren't a good match. After all, no matter how much they loved each other, it didn't change the fact that they ultimately wanted different things, right? Grace wanted a home and a family to fill it with. Hunter wanted no two days to be the same.

Maybe it was for the best that they had gone their separate ways.

And for a while, he had almost believed it.

Some sick part of him had always been curious to see what was more amazing than traveling the world together. What did Darling have that Hunter hadn't?

He glanced around the room. This place wasn't so bad. Definitely cozy. It was more of a home than he had ever given her. Now all that was missing was the family, though maybe it was a little too late for that. They were both closer to their forties than their twenties, after all.

Hunter shifted on the bed, hating the guilty feeling that crept into his stomach. When they'd said their wedding vows, Hunter had never promised Grace a home. He promised to love her forever. That they would have a good life. How the hell was he supposed to know that meant a permanent address and PTA meetings?

Because that's normal.

Oh yeah. That.

Hunter had never wanted normal. He grew up in a small desert town, drowning in normal. All that he had gotten out of that was knowing he wanted something completely different.

And now she was dating? His wife, dating!

Well, his wife for a little while longer, at least. He would sign the divorce papers, of course. It was a lot easier to ignore an email than a living, breathing, pissed-off woman standing right in front of him.

I want to be there when you realize normal isn't what you want at all.

Hunter rested his forearm across his eyes. Why had he said that? Did he really want to stick around while she dated?

Maybe he wanted to know the kind of guy she ended up with, even though he already knew there wouldn't be anyone good enough. Or maybe he hoped if he was standing right there by her side, she'd realize he was the only one for her.

He sat up in bed. Where had that come from? Hunter didn't love Grace anymore. Not like that. He was over it.

Hunter gulped. Or was he?

He could hear conversation downstairs, the roar of the espresso machine. Then it stopped, followed by a curse word.

Hunter smiled to himself. Nice to know he could still get to Grace too.

His phone buzzed, and Hunter fished it out of his pocket. "What's up, Dana?"

"Just checking in. How are you doing?"

Hunter hesitated before deciding that honesty was the best policy. "I don't know."

"You don't know? What do you mean you don't know?"

Hunter swallowed. "I'm not at my place."

He could hear the wheels spinning in her head, the cogs and widgets taking in the new information. "I'm drawing a blank. Where are you?"

Hunter braced himself. "Alaska."

"Alaska? What the—" She breathed into the phone. "Grace."

"Yep."

Dana barked a laugh. "I don't know where to start. The fact that you disappeared on me or that you got all the way to Alaska without realizing what a stupid idea that was."

Hunter blew air through his lips. Dana got annoyed with him at least once a week. It was all part of the brother-sister dynamic they had that made their partnership work. They were more like family than colleagues. "It's not stupid. It's perfect. No one here knows me. Well, almost no one. I needed to get away from it all, and this is the perfect place." He swallowed. "I need a vacation, Dana. My last one didn't go so well."

Tap. Tap. Tap. He could picture her manicured nails clicking on her desk, the Bluetooth stuck to her ear. "Kid, I'm only telling you this because I love you."

Hunter looked up at the ceiling. She always called him kid, even though they were almost the same age. "You love your commission."

"You know me so well," she said dryly, knowing he was joking. "But here's the truth. You lost your aunt, and then what happened to Jack? Well, that's just tragic. I still can't believe you aren't going to the funeral."

Hunter pressed his lips together. There was nothing more to say about that, and she knew it. He was grieving for Jack in his own way. His friend would understand.

"I know you think this is the worst it's ever been for you. But I'm telling you, it's not."

Hunter squirmed at the compassion in her voice. He liked it better when she was being a hard-ass. "What are you talking about?"

"I'm going to get your brain checked out because you've clearly forgotten. When Grace left, you were a total mess."

Hunter clenched his free hand. Dana was wrong. He hadn't been a mess. He hadn't shirked any assignments. Hadn't raged in a hotel room until he was certain security would ask him to leave. Hadn't forgotten how to live. "No, I wasn't."

Dana sighed. "Well, that's decided. I'm scheduling the doctor right now. Maybe a shrink. Because I know you, kid. There is only one person who's ever truly messed you up. And you're there with her right now."

"You're being ridiculous. Grace and I parted ways. It was natural—"

"Save it, because I'm not buying it," Dana interrupted. "I did my job, but we both know you're going to do what you're going to do. Now, about work. These soulless assholes don't care about your broken heart. They want to book you. How long do you need me to hold them off? Tell me, and I'll make it happen."

"I...I'm not sure. I'm going to talk to Grace about it tonight."

Dana chuckled. "I see I'm too late. You're already doomed. Well, I'll drag you out of there kicking and screaming if I have to, otherwise you'll never come back. I'm not letting you do this to yourself, kid. I care too much, inconvenient as that is."

"I wish you could see me rolling my eyes right now."

Loud typing came over the line. "I can imagine."

"What are you working on now?"

"Hmm? Oh, nothing. Just an idea for a TV show if this goes south. *Two Idiots*. What do you think?"

This time, he really did roll his eyes. "Ha-ha. Goodbye, Dana."

Hunter put his phone on airplane mode and set it on the side table. That was enough for one day.

Dana was totally nuts. He was coming back. Yeah, this place was cozy, but not forever. There was nowhere in the world like that for him. He needed movement, change. The closest he ever got to home was traveling the world with Grace by his side. If only she could've understood that. If only that had been enough for her.

Hunter shook it off. Nope. He wasn't going there. Grace had left him. That's what he needed to remember.

Hopefully, Dana wouldn't be too sad when her idea for a TV show didn't come to fruition. People still wanted him for assignments? Great. As soon as he was ready to get out of here, he would throw himself back into work. He'd take magazine layouts, ad campaigns, and every lifestyle piece he could get his hands on.

Work was something that wouldn't leave him one day.

Work was safe. He would be back in the field before Dana knew it. In fact, he should call her right now and ask her to book him something. It wouldn't take him long to go stir-crazy. It never did.

Hunter twisted to reach for his phone again when he caught sight of Ruby. The dog was flopped on her side, her chest rising and falling with each deep breath.

God, he wished he could sleep like that.

Hunter lay back on the bed. Maybe if he just tried to focus on something other than his problems. Maybe if he just cleared his head and listened to the damn dog breathe…

His eyes fluttered open. When had he fallen asleep?

Hunter lifted a hand and rested it on his chest. The tight feeling was gone for now. He could take a deep breath for the first time in a week.

His heart seemed to stop as the realization slammed into him. Suddenly, the answer was obvious.

Jack had known it. Dana had hassled him about it just now. They both knew him better than he knew himself.

Grace was the only one for Hunter. She always had been and always would be. She was the only one who could make things right again.

Sometimes I wish I had done things differently.

Hunter swallowed. Jack might not have the chance to do things differently. But Hunter wouldn't waste his.

It was so easy to see. The solution to all his problems.

Clearly, he and Grace still cared for each other. Why else had neither of them been with someone else in all their years apart? Why else did he run here when he wanted to give up living altogether? And why else had Grace let him stay?

It didn't matter that he hadn't even been here for a full day. For someone who lived in the moment, that was more than enough time to know.

He had never fallen out of love with Grace, and nothing mattered more than being the man she deserved.

A soft knock came at the door, and Grace poked her head in the room. "Hello, sleeping beauty. You hungry?"

His stomach growled at the mention of food. Eating was something else Hunter had fallen out of practice of doing since Jack died. But that, too, seemed to be different with Grace around. "I could eat."

"Let me take Ruby out for a minute, and then we can head to the Buck."

"I take it that's a restaurant?"

"It's the restaurant."

Hunter blinked. *The* restaurant? What had he gotten himself into? "You mean—"

She nodded. "There's only one."

"In that case, sounds great."

"Good. Because we need to talk." She left, closing the door behind her.

Hunter stared at the doorway, his heart pounding in his ears. Oh, they would talk alright. Because he had something to tell her too.

Hunter was going to prove to Grace that their love story wasn't over yet.

CHAPTER SEVEN

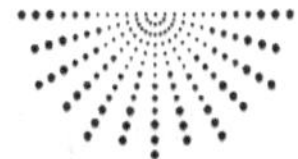

GRACE

Going to the Buck with Hunter went against every instinct in her body. Grace didn't want him getting any ideas. She wasn't being friendly. She wasn't glad to see him.

Just the opposite. Grace needed to set Hunter straight, and this was as close as it got to neutral territory around here.

Wolfie stood behind the bar, greeting them with a smile. "Grace, what a nice surprise. And you brought a friend."

Grace tugged on the hem of her sweater. She didn't have a problem with the friendly barkeep. It was being at the Buckwild Bar and Grill with Hunter that put her on edge. Their appearance at the restaurant would keep the Darling gossip mill churning for days. "This is Hunter. Couldn't let him visit without a drink at the best bar in town."

She decided to leave out the part where Hunter was her husband. Let people think what they wanted. Nothing they came up with could be worse than the truth. Grace and

Hunter were married, though not for much longer if she had anything to say about it.

Hunter reached across the bar, grasping Wolfie's hand. "Nice to meet you."

"Likewise. It's always a pleasure to have new people around here." Wolfie took his hand back, resting it on the beer pull. "Did you two just want a drink? Or can I interest you in dinner?"

Grace practically licked her lips. She definitely needed a glass of wine. But drinking on an empty stomach was a recipe for misery, especially considering the emotional roller coaster she'd been on since Hunter had shown up. "You can count us in for dinner *and* drinks."

Wolfie gestured to the restaurant. "Sit anywhere you like."

They took a booth by the window. Grace sat facing the coffee shop, a reminder of what she was fighting for.

The life she'd created for herself. The life she loved. A life without her husband.

Hunter followed her to the table but didn't sit. He set his hand on her shoulder, and her body warmed at his touch. "I'll be right back."

Grace gritted her teeth. Absolutely not. She wasn't falling for him again. She knew better. He was familiar, that was it. Just a conditioned reaction.

Hunter walked to the bar, his shoulders relaxed as he struck up a conversation with Wolfie.

She let out a huff. Grace wasn't surprised. Hunter had always felt at home anywhere. That's what made it so hard for him to understand her. He didn't get why she needed a home when they had the entire world.

He came back to the table with a beer in each hand, passing one to her. "Cheers."

Grace eyed the foamy pint. "I prefer wine."

"I remember." He took a seat across from her. "But Wolfie

told me he makes the beer himself. Figure we might as well enjoy the local delicacies. Like old times."

Grace shot him a look. This was nothing like old times. She was her own person and made her own decisions now, including what she wanted to drink. But Grace didn't want to hurt Wolfie's feelings by sending the beer back.

She took a small sip, lifting an eyebrow. It was better than she had expected. The yeasty flavor was light and refreshing, and the bubbly brew almost had a floral scent. "Not bad."

"Not bad? This is the only place in town. Don't tell me it's the first time you've tried it."

She shifted in her seat. "I've been here once or twice before."

He gaped at her. "That's it? Do you make an annual visit or something?"

Grace set her beer aside and folded her hands. "I can't close the shop whenever I want. I'm open every day but Sunday. Doesn't leave much time for eating out."

She decided not to mention the part where she felt like a weirdo eating at the restaurant alone. Not that it bothered her to be on her own. But if the pitying looks and encouraging comments she got were any clue, it definitely bothered other people. They had no idea how hard she'd worked to be alone.

Hunter didn't need to know that, though. The less he knew, the better. He had always been able to see right through her, and he didn't need any more ammo.

He picked up one of the floppy plastic menus from the table. "Normally, I'd ask you what's good here."

"You're a big boy," Grace said in a clipped tone. "You can decide for yourself. Besides, I'm still vegetarian."

A smug look passed across his face. "And you think I'm not?"

Grace pursed her lips. "In that case, I can recommend the veggie wrap."

Hunter studied the menu. "With a side salad?"

"With fries," she grumbled.

He grinned. "Finally. Something we can agree on."

Grace took a sip of her beer to hide her smile. How could Hunter annoy her one minute and make her laugh the next? This was exactly why they didn't belong together. He hadn't even been here a full day, and already, she could barely make heads or tails of her own emotions.

Wolfie dropped off their food with a wink, and a blush crawled up her neck. Maybe coming to the Buck hadn't been such a good idea.

Grace half expected Hunter to gag on the veggie wrap. Was he really still a vegetarian two years later? But he finished it in a few quick bites. It should be comforting that he hadn't lied to her yet, but it had the opposite effect. Sometimes the truth hurt worst of all.

He wiped his mouth with a napkin. "Any plans for your birthday? Dinner at the Buck, perhaps? Since it's the only place in town."

Grace stuck out her chin. He never could take anything seriously. "Why does it matter? You won't be here by then."

Hunter had never been good about sticking around one place for very long. Right now, that worked in Grace's favor. She needed her space before she got lost in him again. Before she couldn't find her way back out.

Based on his pained expression, her comment had hit its mark. "I know I screwed up before. I told you, I'm sorry."

Grace pushed her plate aside, her veggie wrap barely touched. Unlike Hunter, she didn't have much of an appetite. Her beer, however, was gone. "Back to business. The attorney I spoke with in Ketchikan said it should be simple, assuming we don't want to change anything about the paperwork. We can be legally divorced within thirty days of filing."

His face paled slightly. "That's it, huh? You can't even try to get along?"

"Trust me. This is me trying."

Trying not to get lost in him again. Trying not to lose herself.

Grace rolled her empty glass between her palms. Did she want another drink? She still preferred wine, but after a day like today, a beer tasted pretty satisfying.

Before she could say anything, Hunter caught Wolfie's eye and signaled for another round.

She gulped. So Hunter could still read her thoughts.

Wolfie dropped off their beers and whisked away their dinner plates. One look at the two of them, and he had the good sense to leave without saying anything.

Wolfie had a talent for knowing exactly what to say and for knowing when to say nothing at all. The barkeep had been a psychologist before he ran the Buck. The way he told it, his time behind the bar had only sharpened his people-reading skills.

Grace trailed her finger down the glass, tracing a path in the frost. "You don't want to stay here. You don't want to hang out in the middle of nowhere with me. You have a dream job. A dream life."

Hunter's gray eyes turned down. "You know I have my reasons for being here."

Her heart softened. She wanted to hate him. But it was hard to unlearn almost two decades of loving someone.

Then she remembered she was going back to her apartment with Hunter, and everything felt impossible again. She could drink a gallon of beer and still not be ready. If Ruby wasn't waiting for her, Grace might never go back. Let Hunter have the place if he needed to be here so badly. Grace just wanted to be left alone. She never intended to share her space again, and definitely not with her husband.

She squared her shoulders. Hunter always had been stubborn. He had to be. Even though he had lucked out with his career, it was still a tough business, and his success was a testimony to his determination. But Grace could be stubborn too. "I know. But I spent years living the life *you* wanted. Now I'm trying to live my own life."

Hunter took a long swallow of his beer, setting down his glass with a thump. "Counteroffer: I'll sign those damn papers. I'll sign whatever you want. But until the divorce is finalized, I stick around Darling. And I'm not staying at the lodge."

Her jaw dropped. It was a tie for which declaration shocked her more. That Hunter had finally agreed to sign the papers or that he wanted to stay here with her. "What? Why?"

Hunter held her gaze. "Because we're meant to be together, Grace. And I want to show you that."

Her heart seemed to stop for a moment. All the feelings came back, slamming into the defenses she had spent the last two years building up like a battering ram. She pressed her hands into the wooden bench, needing something solid to ground her. "You don't mean that. Even if you did, it doesn't matter. We're over. We've been over."

"I told you. I know I screwed up. I can probably never make it right. But at least give me the chance to try."

Grace reached for her beer and took a gulp. Give him a chance? No way. She'd given him fifteen years of chances.

She studied the tiny bubbles dancing in the amber brew. But maybe she could give herself a chance. Grace had been trying for two years to get Hunter to sign the divorce papers. Now, she had leverage. And it wasn't like she wanted Hunter back anyway, right? She had nothing to lose. "If I agree to this, the clock starts when we file the paperwork. Thirty days. Take it or leave it."

The less time, the better. The less time, the less it would hurt when he walked away.

Hunter didn't miss a beat. "Agreed."

"And we're not together. I can still date." She wasn't exactly excited about being on the dating app, but it would be an effective way to send the message loud and clear that she was over Hunter.

"I'll help you."

She narrowed her eyes. "Why would you help me with my love life?"

The corner of his mouth turned up. "Maybe I just want to show you how much dating in your forties sucks. Tip the odds in my favor."

Grace rolled her lips in to keep from smiling. All he had to do to tip the odds in his favor was flash that dimple every once in a while. But she wouldn't let him know that. "And I guess you can date other people too. That's fair."

She didn't love the idea of seeing Hunter with someone else, but who would he date in Darling anyway? Not that she cared. She didn't feel that way about him anymore.

Hunter dipped his chin in apparent agreement. "Anything else?"

Her mind raced, trying to think of all the ways to give herself an advantage. She needed every single one when it came to Hunter. "You can stay with me, but you can't hang around all the time." Grace tapped on the table. "They have Wi-Fi here. This is your new co-working space."

"I've had worse."

Her heart pounded. It had nothing to do with the fact that Hunter still had feelings for her. It was just the excitement of the moment. Grace knew how the story ended with Hunter. There was nothing exciting about that. "And if I don't feel differently by the time the divorce is finalized?"

Hunter spread his hands on the table. "You'll never see me again. I'll leave you alone. Forever."

Grace swallowed. He was offering her what she wanted. Right? To never see him again? Never see his dimple? Never hear his laugh?

She straightened. Of course she wanted that. It was what she'd wanted for the last two years.

"Perfect. The divorce can be my birthday present. I don't think you could get me anything better if you tried." Grace looked him in the eye. "Just don't forget, as far as you and I go, there's nothing going on. We're divorced, or almost divorced. You may still have feelings. I don't. No funny business."

His mouth quirked up. "I won't forget if you don't."

She rolled her eyes. God, he could irritate her. It was almost reassuring. There was no chance of falling back in love with him.

Unless, of course, she had never fallen out of it.

"Now that's decided, you ready to go?" Hunter threw back the rest of his beer before standing and pulling out his wallet.

Grace reached out and grabbed his arm. "You can't pay."

"I insist."

She shook her head. "Look, I'm not trying to be progressive here. What I am saying is that Wolfie won't let you pay. People just leave what they can."

Hunter peeled off a hundred-dollar bill and stuck it under his empty glass. "That should cover it."

Grace stared at the large bill. Hunter had always been generous, even when he barely had a dollar to his name. It was something she had always liked about him. Money and fame hadn't changed that. It seemed time hadn't either.

When she looked up again, Hunter was halfway across the dining room. She turned on her heel and ran after him.

They crossed the street to her shop. Grace unlocked the door, and they plodded up the stairs, where Ruby greeted them with a yip and a shake of her back end. Grace gathered the dog into her arms, watching Hunter.

He stood facing the window, his back to her. "We had something, Grace. I think we still have it."

A tingle traveled through her. It wasn't what Hunter had said. It was the fact that two years later, she still cared about him more than she should. "I'll keep my end of the bargain if you keep yours. Thirty days, Hunter. No promises after that."

Hunter turned, his face drawn. He reached out and touched her arm. "I'm not going to screw this up again. It's going to be different this time. Better. I promise."

Her head felt fuzzy, and she pulled her arm away. She couldn't think straight around Hunter. She never could. Another reason she needed space. "Good night."

Grace let Ruby out one more time and refreshed the dog's water bowl. She whistled, closing the door behind Ruby when she walked into the room. The dog looked at the door and then back at Grace.

She always left the bedroom door open in case Ruby needed a drink of water in the night. Grace was also used to talking to the dog out loud. How many of her habits had to change now that Hunter was here? Already, he was affecting her, rearranging her world bit by bit. "I know, girl. But we aren't alone anymore."

Settling onto her bed, Grace grabbed her laptop and balanced it on her legs. She typed in Hunter's name into the browser, bringing up pages of results.

Every photo of Hunter showed him alone. That was nothing new. Grace had always been in the background. Her entire life had been in the background. And when she most needed to be important, she had once again been swept away.

She looked down at her arm where Hunter had touched her, the skin still warm. Grace rubbed at the spot with her thumb as if trying to erase his touch. Not that it changed anything. One touch, one promise, wasn't enough to undo everything that had happened.

Grace shut the laptop and set it on the nightstand. She turned off the light and cuddled close with Ruby.

A week ago, everything had seemed predictable. Grace could see her life clearly, what the next twenty or thirty or fifty years would be like. Now, she wasn't so sure.

She squeezed her eyes closed and willed herself to sleep. Like Hunter, there were some things she wasn't ready to face.

But Grace knew one thing for sure.

This wasn't a love story. Hunter wasn't her hero.

CHAPTER EIGHT

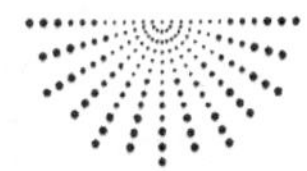

GRACE

Life was strange. Despite Hunter crashing into her world, Grace's morning at the coffee shop hadn't changed a bit.

She got up at the same time, plating pastries and brewing regular and decaf, as always.

At precisely five in the morning, she flicked on the *Open* sign, as always.

Mac came in first thing, as always.

Grace scooped the coffee grounds into the filter for his pour-over. "I know I shouldn't say this to my best customer. But I feel like it would be easier, not to mention cheaper, for you to make coffee at home."

Mac grunted something unintelligible, his gaze lingering on the pastry case.

Grace handed him the steaming mug and grabbed a pair of tongs. "I think that you've earned another free cherry danish by now."

He looked up at her. "Don't tell me you've taken a page out of Wolfie's book. If we don't pay, you don't stay in business. Then I don't have a choice of making coffee at home or not. I want to pay."

Grace slipped the danish into a paper sleeve and passed it across the counter. "And I want to give it to you. Enjoy."

Mac made an expression that might almost be a smile, but the beard made it hard to tell.

Grace bit back a laugh as he walked out of the coffee shop. It never failed to amuse her how the extroverted Elle had ended up with the silent giant. Then again, Grace certainly wasn't a love expert.

She shook her head as she pulled shots of espresso for her Americano. That was the understatement of the year. Her almost-ex-husband was upstairs, trying to make things work between them again before the thirty-day countdown clock to their divorce was up.

A countdown clock that was going to start as soon as the paperwork was filed. Luckily, the attorney had confirmed that an electronic signature was fine, which meant they could get the papers signed today without having to go to Ketchikan.

Life continued as normal until almost seven. Grace had just finished making two caramel hot chocolates when footsteps came from the stairs.

In the annoying way that he always had, Hunter looked fantastic first thing in the morning. His hair was perfectly tousled, and the sleepy look in his eyes only added to his appeal. "Morning."

She shivered. His gravelly voice did things to her body that she would rather not feel. Grace had spent so long using her imagination to picture the heroes in her books that she had forgotten what kind of effect a real-life man could have. *No funny business.* "Good morning. Coffee?"

"Please."

She stepped behind the espresso machine. "Anything in particular?"

"Whatever's easy."

Grace lifted a cup from the rack and positioned it under the airpot. She hesitated for a moment before pulling it away. Even though she didn't want Hunter to get too comfortable around here, she couldn't resist making his favorite drink. Just for his first morning. After that, no more special treatment.

Besides, it was easy to remember his order. It was her favorite too. She pulled a couple of shots of espresso, adding them to the cup with hot water. Grace handed the Americano to Hunter.

He took a careful sip. "That's good."

"I guess all those years of working as a barista paid off."

His fiery brows knit together. "Before I got here yesterday, I hadn't thought about that in a long time."

Grace pressed her lips together as she cleaned out the tamp. Wasn't that ironic? She had supported them with barista work while Hunter had chased his dreams, and now he had the dream life to show for it. But she still spent her days at a coffee shop. Suddenly, Grace remembered why she preferred to get her feels from books. She might have to rely solely on her imagination, but she didn't end up disappointed at the end of the day either.

Anyway, it wasn't like Grace had supported them out of the pure goodness of her heart. She had thought they were working towards something together, towards a life they both wanted. A real home with a real family. But those dreams, like her romance book heroes, only lived in her imagination, never finding their way to real life.

Hunter walked over to the bookshelves. "These are all yours, huh?"

She wiped her hands on her apron and went to stand by

him. "Kind of. People can take one and swap it out when they're done. It goes without saying that there isn't a library or a bookstore in town. This is it."

"You always loved reading. When you had your nose stuck in a book, I had to say something to you three times before you finally heard me." Hunter smiled at her, and his dimple popped out.

She found herself mirroring his smile. *Stop that.* But the old memories were like a warm blanket on a winter day. It was tempting to stay in them forever.

Her stomach turned icy. But they didn't have forever. They barely had a month, and it was past time to move on.

"And now I can actually have a book collection. We didn't have a home to keep one, remember?"

The dimple disappeared. "I remember."

Grace shifted her feet. Falling back in love wasn't just unlikely. It was impossible. But Hunter had never lived by the rules that other people did. He never cared much for normal. "I better get back to work. I already have a pile of dishes."

Hunter gestured to the far wall. "Have you ever thought about moving this space around a little? Maybe a few tables over there?"

She looked in the same direction. Instantly, she could tell it would work better. But she had her pride. Grace refused to let Hunter change anything about her current life, not even the furniture. "No, I like it this way. Don't go trying to change everything. I let you stay here. Isn't that enough?"

"You make it sound like you took me in off the street or something. We're married, remember?"

Grace wished she had given him a cup full of coffee grounds if he was going to be so annoying. Then maybe he wouldn't want to hang around. "Oh, I remember alright. Spent the last two years trying to forget."

Hunter took a deep breath. "I'm going to edit photos. Wi-Fi password?"

"You'll have to ask the Buck what their Wi-Fi password is," Grace said primly.

He gave her puppy-dog eyes. "But I'm jet-lagged. Just this one morning. Please?"

"You're immune to jet lag."

His shoulders sagged. "Fine. I'll get out of here. Just gotta grab my laptop."

Hunter turned towards the stairs.

Her heart squeezed. Maybe he wasn't jet-lagged. But he was still hurting from losing his aunt and Jack. A person didn't process that kind of emotional damage in one night.

"Tequila mockingbird," Grace said before she could stop herself. She had always found it impossible to say no to Hunter, more so when he was in pain. Despite her best intentions, some part of her still wanted to make him happy. "That's the password."

He held her gaze. "You always surprise me, Grace. Even after all this time."

"Then we're even. You showing up gave me the biggest surprise of my life."

He smiled again, evaporating her kneecaps, before heading upstairs.

She shook it off. Stupid dimple.

Grace finished the dishes and started making sandwiches for the lunch rush. They were nothing fancy, but they still sold like hotcakes. Locals raved about them, but Grace didn't let it go to her head. People were probably just happy not to have to make something for themselves.

She sliced tomatoes, telling herself it didn't matter if Hunter worked at the coffee shop for the day or not. He would be gone soon enough. It never took him long to get bored, regardless of what he had said yesterday about wanting to be with her again.

He would be gone, they would be divorced, and she'd be living out her fabulous forties as a single woman. Just like she wanted.

Once Grace had a clearly defined relationship status, it would be easier to interact on the dating app. That was the reason she hadn't been active on it since Hunter had come back. It had nothing to do with that voice or those sleepy eyes.

A loud noise came from overhead, and Grace tensed. What the heck was he doing up there?

She set the bell on the counter and stomped upstairs. Yep, she definitely couldn't wait until Hunter was officially out of her life.

Her annoyance felt justified when she saw he had rearranged her living room. Even more annoying was the fact that the space looked better. God damn him. He always had a talent for seeing things others couldn't. "What the hell is this! Why can't you ever leave things alone?"

Hunter crossed his arms. "Why do you always accept things as they are?"

Grace resisted the urge to scream, the achievement of a lifetime in her opinion. This was *her* place. Not his. Not theirs. "I don't have to explain myself to you."

"I'm just trying to make this space better. I thought I was doing something nice."

The bell sounded. With one last scowl at Hunter, Grace headed back downstairs. She mentally added *Not an impossible pain in the ass* to her dating checklist.

With each step, Grace forced a deep breath, trying to take her blood pressure down a couple of notches. She wanted to get rid of Hunter, not her customers. She actually liked them.

Grace's anger was replaced with surprise when she reached the bottom step. She had never seen the petite, older woman standing in front of the counter before. In a town this small, that almost never happened. "Hi, how can I help you?"

The woman's blue eyes rounded with apparent concern. "Are you okay, honey? You seem upset."

Grace gave her a tight smile. She wasn't in the mood to talk about her personal problems, and definitely not with a stranger. "I'm fine."

The woman nodded as if she understood. "Not everyone gets a second chance. But it's always been my belief that everyone deserves one."

Grace scrunched her eyebrows together. How could this stranger have any idea what she was going through? "I'm sorry?"

The woman smiled. "I'm Natasha. Nice to finally meet you, Grace."

A chill fell over Grace. She knew of Natasha. Everyone in Darling knew of her. Except Natasha almost never came to town.

Grace had heard the stories, of course. Two missing children. A husband who had passed away. The ability to know things she should not know. At times, Grace wondered if this was a real person at all or just a legend. Some places had Sasquatch. Darling had a granny psychic.

"How can I help you?" Grace asked again. She was already dealing with too many impossible problems. Solving the mystery of Natasha would have to wait for another day.

Natasha's gaze zigzagged across the menu. "A hot chocolate would be nice. And a double fudge cookie." She giggled. "That's probably too much sugar, but I think I don't really care at this point in life."

Grace poured milk into the frothing tin, the roar of the steaming wand mercifully making conversation impossible. She normally liked chatting with her customers. But what was a person supposed to say to someone who was supposedly psychic? Wasn't it kind of pointless?

She sprinkled chocolate shavings on the whipped cream tower and handed Natasha the cup, along with a warmed cookie in a paper sleeve. "Enjoy. Vivian bakes all the cookies, and they're amazing."

Natasha paid and headed towards the door. When she had one foot outside, she paused and turned to look at Grace. "Isn't there anything you want to ask?"

"Ask?"

Natasha smiled patiently, saying nothing.

Grace could hear her own heartbeat. If the rumors were true, Natasha would know what Grace couldn't guess at. But was the truth scarier than not knowing at all? "When will everything be back to normal again?"

The older woman tsked. "That's not what you really want to know. The question is, when will you have what you want?"

Grace's eyes burned. It was a question she hadn't been brave enough to ask herself. She had stopped hoping for what she wanted a long time ago.

"What if you already have everything you ever wanted?" Natasha winked.

The door swung shut, leaving Grace by herself. What the heck was that supposed to mean?

Another loud noise came from above, and Grace's shoulders climbed to her ears. No way she had what she wanted. She didn't want Hunter here. It hadn't been her lifelong dream to run a coffee shop in Alaska. She didn't want to be less than a month away from forty and still figuring life out.

But it was too late for some things. Grace had accepted that not everyone got a happy ending in life. Some people had to be happy with good enough.

With a sigh, Grace went upstairs once again to see what the hell Hunter was changing this time.

CHAPTER NINE

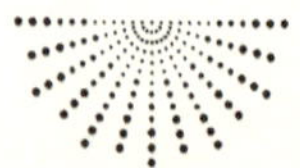

HUNTER

Footsteps pounded on the wooden staircase. Hunter grabbed his laptop from the kitchen table and ducked into his bedroom. He felt like a coward for hiding, but so far, his plan to win Grace back wasn't going well. Hunter knew he couldn't expect to erase fifteen years of history in only one night. If he could, he'd do it and leave just the good parts.

But everything Hunter did only seemed to upset Grace more. It wasn't just frustrating. It was disheartening. Once upon a time, he had known her as well as he knew himself.

At first, he thought it was a good sign that she had let him stay and work at the coffee shop. But every time he made so much as a peep, Grace would march upstairs to question him. He had no idea what to do. Old Grace had loved spending time around Hunter. New Grace held him at arm's length and acted like it wasn't far enough.

He shifted on the bed, trying to ignore the feeling that he deserved it and worse.

Hunter didn't exactly help his case just now either. Grace

had given an inch by letting him work here for the day, and he had taken a mile by rearranging the furniture. But it wasn't his fault that the place was a mess. The feng shui was all wrong.

It was his Aunt Linda who had first gotten him turned on to feng shui. Her belief in the ancient practice was one of a hundred things that made her a misfit in the small western town where they had lived.

One thing was for sure. Hunter wasn't so worried about Grace dating anymore. The woman had blocked every possible flow of energy in her home. It was a miracle she could even sleep through the night.

After he rearranged the space as best he could, his shoulders finally relaxed. At least until he looked at his computer.

Hunter was an artist, a free agent, a rogue. He answered to no one. But he didn't get to where he was by blowing people off or missing deadlines. He was supposed to have these photos to the editor already. Except he had gotten next to nothing done since Jack had passed away.

Dana had called the magazine and negotiated an extension. She had told Hunter to let her know if he needed more time. Though she hadn't said anything, he doubted the magazine would give him a second chance. They were going to print at the end of the week. Hunter needed to pull himself together before his life completely fell apart.

But every time he opened up his laptop and clicked on the file, the photos reminded him that a little more than a week ago, Jack had still been alive.

Hunter had lost people before. He had never known his parents, not really. They died in a car accident when he was too young to even remember their faces. His aunt had raised him. Then, he had lost her right before Jack.

Guilt settled heavily in his stomach. When Aunt Linda got sick, Hunter had wanted to take care of her himself, but he had been too busy with work. Or at least he had thought he had been too busy. The truth was he'd chosen work over her.

Still, Hunter had tried to do the right thing. Aunt Linda had spent her whole life dreaming of paradise, and Hunter had made that happen for her before her illness. And he had paid for his aunt to have the best care possible at an assisted living home in Hawaii, where she'd retired.

Hunter stared at the computer screen. He wasn't to blame for his parents or his aunt, and he wasn't to blame for what happened with Jack either.

But none of that logic changed the fact that while Hunter's career had flourished, his personal relationships had withered away. One by one, he had lost them all.

It wasn't like that had been his plan. Hell, he hadn't had a plan. He never had a plan. But that was about to change, starting with his wife.

He wouldn't get a second chance with anyone. Except for Grace. And Hunter didn't intend to screw things up this time.

A knock came at the door.

"I see you kept moving the furniture," Grace's muffled voice said.

He sighed. "I'll put it back if you want."

"Actually, it looks nice. And if you're hungry, there is a sandwich waiting for you downstairs."

Hunter stood and opened the door. "Really? You like the furniture?"

Grace glanced back at the living space. "I do. It feels better."

It wasn't much. But it was something. "A sandwich sounds good."

She peered at him. "You never take a break when you're editing. What's wrong?"

His stomach churned. For so long, photography seemed like the only thing he could do right. Now, Hunter wondered if he'd ever be able to do it again. "Those photos are hard for me to look at."

She bit her lip. "Let's look at them together, then. The Wi-Fi signal is better downstairs, anyway."

A spark of hope flickered to life inside his heart. Maybe she didn't hate him as much as she said. "You sure?"

Grace nodded. "We can sign the papers at the same time. If I get them to the attorney today, he should be able to file within a day or two."

The spark spurted and went dark. Oh. The divorce. Right.

She grabbed her laptop from the kitchen table, and Hunter followed her downstairs with his own laptop in hand.

His feet felt heavier with each step. Defrosting his wife was proving to be more slow going than his editing.

Once they were downstairs, Grace ducked behind the counter. "Caprese okay?"

"Caprese is great." He didn't have much of an appetite, but Hunter would take any peace offering she gave him. Today, that came in the form of a tomato-and-cheese sandwich.

Grace set out two plates, using tongs to set a sandwich on each one. She added a small side salad, drizzling olive oil and balsamic vinegar over the fluffy lettuce.

He peeked over the counter to get a better look. "No chips?"

She snapped the tongs at him. "We had fries last night, mister. Life is about balance."

Hunter laughed and followed her to one of the bistro tables. He dug into the salad first. For a guy in a sorry state, eating his greens seemed like a good place to start.

The salad was simple but delicious. The sandwich was

even better. The tomatoes were fresh and juicy, and the mozzarella creamy.

His stomach growled as his appetite came to life. Already, he had eaten more after one day in Darling than he had the entire last week.

Once they had finished, Grace cleared their plates and brought over a glass of iced tea for each of them. "Ready when you are."

Hunter took a deep breath before opening the laptop. He selected the file, angling the computer towards Grace so that she could see the screen too.

After the first couple of pictures, the basil taste turned sour in his mouth. It didn't matter what the photos were of. All he saw was Jack falling to the ground over and over again.

Hunter clicked through as fast as he could. He considered it a success when he made it to the end without barfing up his sandwich.

Grace leaned back in her chair. "Those are amazing. I don't see why you need to edit them at all."

Hunter gave her a small smile. She had always seen the best in him. Until she hadn't. "I appreciate it, but trust me, if I submitted these to the magazine now, they would consider it garbage."

She wrinkled her nose. "Right. The magazine. Even after all this time, I forget you're famous sometimes. To me, you're still just that broke kid from college."

"I'm sorry—"

"Don't be. I left you, remember?"

He winced. How could he forget? How could he not remember the beginning of the end?

Grace jumped to her feet. "I'll get my laptop so we can sign the papers."

She stepped behind the counter and grabbed her

computer. Grace couldn't have sent a clearer message if she had written it on neon poster board.

Conversation over.

Grace brought the laptop over, opening up the screen and pointing. "The boxes that need your signature are highlighted in yellow. Once you set it up, you should be able to just paste it in as you go."

His heart ached as he scrolled through the document. Grace had already filled in her signature.

The only thing that kept him from totally falling apart was remembering that it wasn't all over yet. Just because they were signing the paperwork didn't mean they would get divorced. Grace had agreed to let him stay here for a month. That had to mean something.

Hunter finished signing and passed the laptop back to her. "All done."

"Thanks. I'll get these over to him right now before I finish cleaning up."

"Need help with anything?"

She shook her head. "No, thanks. I'm used to doing it on my own."

Hunter said nothing. How could he argue with the truth? He couldn't. He would just have to do better moving forward.

Taking a deep breath, Hunter looked back at his computer. This was not the time to lose it. His emotions were rattled from memories of Jack and all his feelings about Grace. Right now, the best thing he could do was throw himself into work.

He went through the pictures a second time, surprised he was able to stomach looking at them. The pain was still there but dulled, as if Grace had sucked the poison out of his veins. The task no longer seemed impossible.

Hunter glanced up at her. "You really don't mind if I work down here?"

"Not today." She gave him a pointed look. "Just don't get used to it."

He nodded. Right, of course. She had only made an exception for one day. For one month. In her eyes, this was all temporary. But not if he could change that.

Hunter zoned in on his computer, letting the work consume him. Editing required his complete focus. He took his art seriously. He had built his life on it. There was no such thing as good enough for him when it came to photography. There was only perfection.

Even all this time later, Grace seemed to still understand that and let him be.

She was too good for him. Always had been.

The next time he looked up, Grace was locking the door and flicking off the *Open* sign. How long had he been working? No wonder years of his life had passed by without him noticing until he looked back.

Grace glanced at Hunter as she walked by. "You're welcome to stay downstairs. The Wi-Fi signal really is better."

"What are you doing?"

"What I always do." As if he was supposed to somehow magically know what that was.

He shifted in his seat, once again reminded of the gap between the Grace he used to know and the Grace in front of him now. He still loved her just as much. What bothered him was that it was his fault she had become a stranger.

Hunter stayed put at the bistro table while Grace went upstairs. It took everything he had not to follow her around like a puppy. She came back down a few minutes later, having changed into warmer clothes. Ruby walked ahead of her on a leash.

Grace gave a little wave as they stepped outside. "See you later."

Hunter resisted the urge to leap from his chair and press his nose to the window to see what Grace was doing. For one, that was creepy. For two, he had to get the photos done, even if it meant working all night. Except he couldn't focus anymore. It was different without Grace.

Hunter ran a hand through his hair. He had forgotten how much easier everything seemed with her around. How much better. He spent the past two years telling himself he didn't need anyone.

Anyone except Grace.

But what if she didn't need him anymore?

CHAPTER TEN

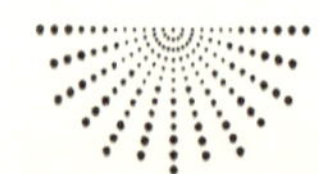

GRACE

Her phone vibrated, and the screen lit up. Grace dragged her gaze back to the pan on the stove and kept stirring. Risotto waited for no one. Not even a cute guy.

Her phone beeped again, and Grace twitched.

Maybe it was the feng shui, but the same day that Hunter had rearranged the furniture, she had gotten a match on the dating app. Three days later, she was still talking to the guy.

Grace had braced herself for one-word answers and inappropriate pictures. She wasn't expecting to actually like him.

So far, Matt seemed normal. He lived in Juneau. He was a CPA. He liked hiking.

Normal. Just like she wanted.

She couldn't wait to tell Vivian. Grace might end up going on a date before her fortieth birthday after all.

A third beep. She gripped the wooden spoon with one hand, the other clenched in a fist. The last thing she wanted to do was to text Matt when Hunter was around. She felt awkward enough dating at her age, let alone when her husband was living with her.

Or, as he would be known twenty-eight days from now, her ex-husband.

Hunter wandered into the kitchen. Speak of the devil. "Ruby is conked out in the living room, so I came in here to see if the company was any better. Can I help with dinner?"

She held the spoon out to him. "Stir, please."

Hunter sniffed the pot. "Risotto, my favorite." He shot her a playful smile. "Are you trying to seduce me, Grace?"

She grabbed her phone from the counter. "Don't make me throw the whole thing in the trash."

Plunking herself down in a kitchen chair, Grace focused on keeping a straight face as she scrolled through Matt's messages. No need to give Hunter any clues that she was texting with a guy. She would quickly reply to Matt, then take over cooking again.

"Um, Grace? Grace?" Hunter waved his hand in front of her face.

"What?" she snarled. Couldn't he make it five seconds without bugging her?

Hunter stepped back. "Easy there, tiger. I just wanted to let you know the food is done."

She frowned. That wasn't possible. "Done? But that recipe takes half an hour."

He chuckled. "Yeah. You've been zoned out for a while. I gave up on conversation about fifteen minutes ago. Care to share what is so fascinating?"

She stood to set the table, hoping she wasn't blushing. This was why she only texted with Matt in between coffee orders during the day. Hunter was at the Buck then, where he wasn't able to read her like a book. "Nope."

Hunter smirked. "Oh God. Don't tell me it's a boy. I told you. Feng shui works."

"A man, thank you very much." Grace pressed her lips together. Drat. Now he knew.

Hunter held out a hand. "I need to see this guy."

She clutched her phone to her chest. "Are you insane? No way! My ex-husband is not the gatekeeper."

"Correction." Hunter waggled a finger. "Current husband. Does lover boy know that?"

She shoved her phone into her pocket and walked over to the silverware drawer. "As far as he's concerned, you're my ex."

"What's his story? Wife left him? Single dad? Does he need a sugar mama?"

The spoons clattered as Grace tossed them on the table. "Why? Because someone our age who is single has to have something wrong with him? Does that mean there is something wrong with me? Or you?"

Hunter held up his hands. "Whoa. You really like this guy, huh? Let me help. I promised I would, remember?"

"The only help you could provide would be your life story as a manual for what not to do."

"Ouch." Hunter splayed his hand against his chest in mock pain. "Can we call a truce for dinner? Or did you put rat poison in the risotto?"

Holding back a laugh, Grace spooned the creamy rice into bowls, setting them on the table. Only Hunter could both piss her off and crack her up in the same second. He drove her crazy. One of the many reasons they didn't belong together, no matter what he thought. "There's nothing to tell. He's a perfectly normal guy. We've only been talking for a few days. Nothing worth a ferry ride yet."

Hunter fluttered his eyelashes dramatically. "Ah, a ferry ride. The sign of true love in Alaska."

She pointed her spoon at him. "You laugh, but stick around and you'll see."

He held her gaze, his playful expression gone. "I plan on it."

She swallowed, her mouth suddenly dry. Grace stuck her spoon into her bowl. She wasn't attracted to Hunter anymore. She was talking to another guy, for goodness' sake.

"You know what we need? Conversational lubricant." Hunter stood and made his way to the pantry, pulling out a bottle of pinot grigio. "I knew I saw something in here earlier. Do you mind?"

A glass of wine was one of the few things she could agree on with Hunter. Maybe two glasses at this rate. "Please do the honors."

He opened the wine and handed her a healthy pour. "Now. Tell me everything. How can I help if I don't know what I am helping with?"

She took a sip of the wine, her shoulders relaxing a smidge. "He's just, I don't know, normal. He lives in Juneau. Not married. Never has been."

"What does he do for work?"

"He's an accountant."

Hunter snorted. "Perfect. He can help organize your financial affairs for when you die an early death due to the boredom of dating an accountant."

"You're just in denial that anyone could want a life different from yours. People like normal, Hunter. That's why it's called normal."

"You can't honestly want that."

Grace narrowed her eyes. "Are we having this conversation or not?"

"I'm sorry. Please continue. I'll keep my commentary to myself."

With a pointed look and another sip of wine, Grace told Hunter what she knew about Matt. He was perfect.

Or at least he would be if he had a dimple. That part she kept to herself.

Hunter leaned back in his chair. "So, you really like this guy?"

"I mean, it's only been three days of talking. Who knows?"

"Well, I know you. You don't take love lightly. But when you fall, you fall hard."

Grace rested her chin on her hand, studying Hunter. He should know. Since the day she had met him, there had been no one else. Even now, she wasn't sure there ever would be. Matt was fun to talk to, but Grace wasn't looking to get married again. She liked her life the way it was. Mostly. "I just hope I can get through the first date. It's been a couple of decades since I've been on one."

"Just be yourself." Hunter rubbed his stomach. "And maybe make him this recipe sometime. It was even better than I remembered. Is he vegetarian too?"

"I don't know." She grabbed her phone and shot off a quick message. It beeped only a few seconds later. "Yes!"

Hunter rolled his eyes. "Or so he says. You know how to find out what a guy really thinks, right?"

"There's a way to find out?"

He leaned in. Grace could see the midnight-blue specks in his gray eyes, the faint freckles on his forehead. She could smell that musky scent that was always part of him, even in the middle of a damn jungle.

Her pulse fluttered, and she gulped. Wasn't she literally talking to another guy right now?

Stupid biology.

"Ask him after," Hunter said, his voice low.

"After?"

"You know. After you sleep together."

Grace recoiled. "You're disgusting."

"Don't believe me? Before then, the guy only has one goal

in mind. And if it means pretending to be vegetarian, so be it."

She swirled her wine, watching the legs trail down the glass. "I don't see us getting that far. I'm not looking for anything serious right now."

"Finally, some good news." He picked up the dirty dishes and walked to the sink.

Grace stared at him. Hunter wasn't jealous, was he? The man had the confidence of a rock star. He didn't get jealous.

But if he was, she didn't totally hate it. Truth be told, it felt kind of good.

Turning on the water, he scrubbed the dishes and set them in the drying rack, his perfect backside on display.

Her face warmed, and Grace begged her body to get its head on straight. Hunter wasn't the one she cared about. He wasn't the one she was interested in.

So what if his jeans still hung off him perfectly? Who cared if she still found the scent of him delicious? Grace knew where things would go with Hunter. At best, nowhere. At worst, she'd lose herself again.

She forced her gaze back to her phone. Matt was sweet and funny and had that rare quality: potential. Matt was the guy she should be feeling fluttery over. Matt was the hero. Hunter was the villain. End of story.

"So, when are you going to see him?" Hunter asked.

Grace looked up, trying to ignore how damn sexy he looked as he leaned against the counter and dried his hands. It didn't seem physically possible that the outline of his abs should be visible under his T-shirt. Clearly, she needed to go on a date. And fast. Grace was in desperate need of a Hunter detox. "Don't know. He hasn't asked yet."

Her phone buzzed again, and Hunter arched an eyebrow. "I don't think it'll be too long. He sounds like a man who knows what he wants."

Her chest tightened. It was all too much too fast. The date. Turning forty. Hunter in her home. She held out her wineglass. "Any chance I could get a refill?"

"Of course." He tipped the bottle over her glass before refilling his own. "Shall we finish this conversation in the living room?"

"What conversation?"

"This Matt guy. I want to help."

She stood from the table. "No, thanks. I don't need a male perspective."

"And you think that's what I'm trying to do?"

"Isn't it?"

Hunter pinned her with his gaze. "Honey, I already told you what I'm all about. There's only one guy for you, and you're looking at him."

CHAPTER ELEVEN

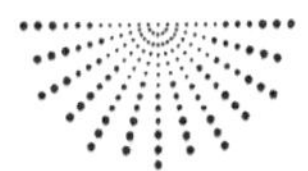

HUNTER

They really should give Hunter an Academy Award. Because he was doing an incredible job of playing it cool.

Not that he cared about the stupid dating app. Nope. No way. Hunter knew that he and Grace belonged together. Some asshat from Juneau wasn't going to change that.

A boring asshat.

An accountant.

Hunter practically fell asleep just saying the word.

Besides, Grace was a grown woman. If she wanted to go on a date, then by all means, she should go. It actually worked in Hunter's favor. He had wanted to prove that dating at this age sucked. Based on the sound of this guy, he would do all the work for Hunter.

But wasn't it natural for a man to feel a little defensive about his wife losing her head over a new guy? Even if he knew it was going nowhere? He had almost dropped to his knees and said a prayer of thanks when Grace had mentioned she had no plans to sleep with the guy.

Hunter took another sip of wine. Protective. That was it. He was feeling protective. After all, he had given Grace his whole heart for almost two decades.

And maybe it hurt a little bit that this guy seemed to be the exact opposite of Hunter, and that's why Grace was so interested. She really didn't have to throw that in his face, did she?

Hunter was momentarily tempted to move the furniture back and block the energy flow again. It might mess with his karma a little, but maybe it would be worth it.

Grace turned from him and walked to the living room, but not before he saw the color in her cheeks. Interesting. Did he still affect her the same way she did him? "You had your chance, Hunter. Fifteen years of chances. Let someone else have a turn."

His shoulders slumped forward slightly. Maybe not.

He followed her, doubling down on his resolve to get things right with Grace. He could see Jack laughing now, smug with the satisfaction that he had been right about Hunter and Grace all this time.

Hunter sat down on the sofa, where Ruby promptly jumped into his lap. He let out a sigh. Weren't dogs supposed to be intuitive? So why couldn't the fluffball sense he wasn't a fan of canines? But Hunter couldn't bring himself to move the little dog. "Assuming this guy even deserves a turn. What kind of stuff does he like?"

"Travel, hiking—"

Hunter made a barfing motion. "I swear to God, if you say tacos. Did he copy and paste this off some sort of dating app template or something?"

Grace rolled her eyes. "I feel like we've had this conversation a million times. Not all of us can have your résumé." She deepened her voice. "'Hunter Hart. You've probably seen my work because I'm famous. My life is better than your vacation. Also, I'm hot.'"

He grinned. "Nice to know you think I'm still hot."

Grace stuck her tongue out at him. "The joke is on you. That was from your perspective, remember?"

"Let me guess yours. 'Grace Hart. Happily divorced. Dog mom. Entrepreneur.'"

She laughed. "You nailed it."

"That's not what I would write for you, though."

Grace tilted her head. "Oh yeah? What would you put?"

"Super smart. Natural beauty. Loyal to a fault."

"That's really what you think?" Her voice was quiet.

"Always have."

Grace held his gaze. How long they sat like that, he didn't know. Hunter wanted to say more. To tell her everything. To show her his entire heart if it meant she would finally believe him. But Hunter knew it was too late for words. He would have to prove to Grace with actions how much she meant to him. But what exactly?

Ruby nuzzled his hand and brought him back to earth. Okay. Maybe he did like dogs. Or at least this one. She made him feel slightly less hopeless about life. "Back to Matt or whatever his name is. Please let me help you."

"And what if it backfires? What if I like him so much that I divorce you and then marry him?"

Hunter's throat tightened. Then he really would've lost everything. But he didn't want to sound totally desperate. Yet. "We have a deal, remember? Once the divorce is finalized, *if* the divorce is finalized, then I'm gone forever. So shoot me if I want to make sure the person keeping you company isn't a piece of shit."

"That's very noble of you, but just because I'm alone doesn't mean I'm lonely. And trust me, I know how to spot an asshole."

Guilt curled in his stomach as the Academy Award slipped from his grasp. "I'm guessing you learned that from me."

"That's what you really think, huh? That I blame you? I'm the one I'm mad at, Hunter. I wasn't brave when I needed to be. I didn't stand up for what I wanted."

His mouth turned dry. "Was it really all bad, Grace?"

Her gaze dropped to her lap. "No, it wasn't all bad. Like it or not, you were the love of my life."

Hunter forgot how to breathe for a moment, her words a sucker punch to the stomach. *Were*. Past tense.

Trying to pull himself together, Hunter set his wineglass down. That shit was making him emotional, and this wasn't the time to lose his head. Not when he had a marriage to save.

If he could save it. If he didn't run out of time. He had already been here for several days, and besides that first morning, Grace had stuck to her guns about Hunter working at the Buck.

It wasn't that Hunter didn't like working there. He enjoyed chatting with Wolfie and the other friendly locals who wandered in throughout the day. But it didn't exactly give him ample opportunities to remind Grace how good they had been together either.

He swallowed. He couldn't throw in the towel yet. Jack had run out of time. Hunter would be damned if he did too.

Clapping his hands together, he stood, which earned him an annoyed look from Ruby. "Matt likes hiking. Why don't we go for a hike on your next day off? Get some cute photos of you?"

Grace shuddered. "You'd have better luck finding a unicorn. A good photo of me doesn't exist. You should know."

His heart squeezed. The only thing that killed him more

than the idea of Grace ending up with someone else was hearing her hate on herself. Didn't she know how amazing she was? "Stop it with the negative self-talk. I, madam, am an artist. If anyone can get a good photo of you, it's me."

"You don't have to do this. I've got photos."

Hunter spread his hands in the air. "We'll make you the dating profile to end all dating profiles."

Grace fought a smile. "Seriously, Hunter. I'm already talking to someone. We're kind of past the point of first impressions."

"It might not work out with Matt. Then you'll be back on the market and wanting to put your best foot forward."

She tilted her head. "I'm confused. I thought you wanted to get back together. Now you're helping me snag a new guy?"

He took a deep breath, hoping the next thing he said didn't actually kill him. But he had promised her things would be different this time. Now Hunter actually had to show her. "I may have let you down during our marriage, Grace. But I will not let you down in divorce."

Her dark eyes searched his. "Are you serious? This doesn't seem normal."

He lifted the corner of his mouth. "You know how I feel about normal."

She looked down at her jeans, picking at the fabric. "I suppose it would be nice for you to use your powers for good."

"So it's settled? We'll start with a hike and some photos. What other people can say that they had an award-winning photographer do their dating profile?"

"It's amazing you can fit inside the door with that ego," she commented dryly. "Speaking of photography, don't you have to get back to work soon?"

Hunter shifted his stance. Yeah. And he was trying not to think about it. "Dana is handling things. I have time."

Grace's expression softened. Hunter wasn't surprised. His manager and his wife had always gotten along well. It was one of the million things that he thought made their life perfect. And one of the million things that had made it all the more shocking when Grace had walked away. "I'm glad you still have Dana. She's great."

"Better than I deserve. Seems to be a theme in my life."

Grace sighed. "Fine. Let's take some photos. You might as well make yourself useful while you're here. I won't have this opportunity forever."

He forced a smile. They wouldn't run out of time. Not if he could help it. "This will be fun."

Oh yeah, he had a firm hold on that Academy Award.

CHAPTER TWELVE

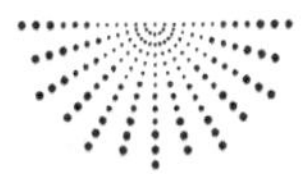

HUNTER

When he had originally suggested going for a hike, Hunter had no idea that he would fall in love. Thick, green branches. A constant mist. The feeling that the sky was closer somehow. It was a rainforest unlike any other he had seen before, and he had seen almost all of them in the world.

Hunter's neck ached from looking up. They had been walking for hours, and he was still in awe of the forest scenery.

Up ahead, Grace picked her way along the trail while Ruby ran around, letting out happy barks. It was impossible not to smile watching the furball enjoy herself.

After a few more photos, his camera beeped a warning. Hunter shielded it from the rain with his jacket and switched out the memory card.

With his camera ready to go, Hunter hurried to catch up with Grace. "Hold up. This spot is perfect."

She turned to face him, the corners of her mouth tugged

down. "We must have hundreds of photos of me by now. Do we really need any more?"

"Trust me. I'm a professional."

With a groan, she stomped over to him. "I thought you preferred landscapes."

"It's sweet you still remember. But desperate times and all that."

Grace glared at him. "I'm not desperate."

"Of course not." He was the one who was desperate. That could be the only reason he offered to help the woman he loved with her dating profile.

He had told Grace it was his chance to prove to her how much dating at this age sucked, but that was bullshit. Hunter wasn't worried about who Grace would end up with. It was the possibility that she would end up with someone at all that terrified him.

His stomach twisted. But it wasn't fair to keep her from living life just because he wasn't ready. Either he had to show Grace that he was the man for her, or he had to be ready to let her go by the time their divorce was finalized. The only problem was that he didn't think he'd ever be ready to let Grace go.

"Alright, I release you." He waved his hand. "Let's keep going."

Grace immediately abandoned the pose and turned, taking long strides along the narrow forest trail. She had always been self-conscious about her height. Hunter found her mile-long legs hot as hell. But then again, he found everything about Grace hot as hell.

The years apart had done nothing to change that. He doubted any amount of time would ever change his feelings about Grace. Too bad he had been too stupid to realize it sooner.

His stomach growled. The croissant he gobbled down this

morning seemed like a distant memory. "Any chance lunch is soon?"

"Getting tired?" Though her back was turned to him, Hunter could hear the smile in her voice.

"Hungry."

"We're almost there." Grace ducked behind a tree, and Hunter followed her.

Suddenly, they weren't in the forest anymore.

Hunter steadied himself, teetering on the edge of a bank facing the Alaskan sea.

Grace tugged on her backpack straps. "What do you think?"

The forest surrounded the beach, making it feel like a seat on the edge of the world. Small waves lapped at the rocky shore. It felt like they were the last two people on Earth.

His heart hiccupped. If they were, there was no one else that Hunter would rather be with. "It's beautiful."

"I thought you might like it."

Hunter held out his hand, feeling at the air. "There's no wind."

"The islands that surround this one protect it from the wind. But this beach, in particular, is very quiet."

Ruby shot past them and scrambled down the rocky shore, barking at the waves.

Hunter chuckled. "Not very quiet today."

They followed Ruby's path down to the beach. A giant piece of driftwood made the perfect spot to sit. A small ring with charred wood sat in front of it.

Hunter looked up at the clouds. "A fire would be nice right about now."

"Maybe next time."

He bit the inside of his cheek to keep from smiling. That was an interesting contradiction to Grace's usual wish for him to leave Darling as soon as possible. It wasn't exactly a grand declaration of love, but he would take what he could get.

Grace handed him a sandwich and a bag of chips. "There are snickerdoodle cookies for dessert."

"My favorite." He took a bite of the sandwich. Pepper jack cheese. Another favorite. Was it a coincidence? Or a love note in food form?

Grace unwrapped her own sandwich. "It wasn't on purpose."

His shoulders sagged. So much for that theory. "Is this what you normally do on your days off?"

"Sometimes. I always take Ruby for a long walk. Read. Stuff like that."

He tilted his head. "By yourself?"

"Why not?"

Hunter took another bite of his sandwich. *You don't miss me?* "You don't get lonely?"

She lifted her shoulder. "Like I said, being alone is different from being lonely. But enough about me. What's your plan?"

"Plan?"

Grace opened her bag of chips. "We both know you can't do your job from here. Dana is great, but you're kind of a critical component to the whole Hunter Hart business model. Eventually, you have to leave."

He crumpled up the parchment paper from his sandwich, regretting that he'd gobbled up the whole thing so quickly when his stomach turned over. The last thing he wanted to talk about was the possibility that this would come to an end. Again. "Do I? I am sure we can figure something out. If anyone can, it's Dana."

Grace gave him a sideways glance. "Until you get bored."

He rested his hands against the driftwood, needing something solid to hold on to. "No, I won't. I love you, Grace. I want to be with you."

She looked out at the dark waves, her face strained. "You love your job. We both know that."

Hunter wished he could go back ten minutes in time, when this had just been a hike. Before they remembered everything that stood between them.

He dusted his hands. Hunter wasn't ready to give up yet. He might never be ready. But if these were going to be his last memories of Grace, he wanted them to be good ones. "Should we take a picture of the two of us? One for the scrapbook?"

Grace's face soured. "Please, no more photos."

"Why do you hate taking pictures so much?"

She gestured to herself. "Look at me. Not all of us can be the handsome and exciting Hunter Hart."

"Nonsense. I'm the least photogenic man on the planet. You'll look great next to me."

He pulled his collapsible tripod out of his backpack and set it up a few feet away. Hunter connected his camera and set the timer before running back to the log. "We have ten seconds!"

Hunter wrapped his arm around Grace's shoulders. The camera flashed, and he gave her a squeeze. "A memory of our reunion."

Grace snorted as she scooted away. "It's still a touchy subject."

They sat there for a few more minutes until Ruby tired herself out running back and forth, chasing the waves.

"I'm going to have to carry her home," Grace joked as they packed up from their picnic, careful not to leave any trash behind.

With a full stomach, the hike back felt easier, and they were back at the Driftwood in no time.

After a hot shower, Hunter flopped onto his bed and uploaded the photos to his computer. He smiled to himself as he clicked through the images. As always, his favorite shots were of Grace.

Hunter had seen more than his fair share of beautiful women in his lifetime. It was an occupational hazard of being a lifestyle photographer. But none of them had ever compared to his wife.

There was something about her bare face. That she only smiled when she meant it. Her ability to be comfortable being on her own. It blew his mind that she didn't realize how gorgeous she truly was, inside and out.

As he edited the photos, he found himself back in his flow. The knot in between his shoulders came undone. So he hadn't lost his work mojo after all.

There was only one person responsible, of course. Grace. She didn't just make everything better. She brought out the best in him.

Over the past couple of years, Hunter had found lots of reasons to love being single. It was easier to travel. He could make last-minute decisions. Hell, he could do whatever he wanted. And suddenly, every single reason he had come up with seemed flimsy.

Hunter kept clicking until he got to the photo of them together on the beach. The angle wasn't perfect. The exposure needed work. But he still loved it.

His throat tightened, and he closed the laptop. Why hadn't he taken more photos with the love of his life over the years?

A knock came at the door.

Hunter cleared his throat. "Come in."

Grace peeked into the room. "I was just about to pour myself a glass of wine. Would you like one?"

"If you insist." He smiled. "Besides, I have something to show you."

She drew her eyebrows together. "What is it?"

Guilt jabbed at him. Life had taught Grace surprises were a bad thing. No doubt he had been part of that too. "I'll be right out."

Hunter put a few final touches on the photo and carried his laptop to the kitchen. He set it on the table. "Check that out."

Grace leaned over, the collar of her pajama top gaping open. He looked away, hoping she didn't notice the flush to his cheeks. *Focus.*

She blinked at the photo. "It's us."

"You don't like it?"

"It's not that. I do like it."

"I'll email you a copy."

She straightened and smiled at him. "Thank you."

Hunter turned in a half circle, taking in the empty walls. "Not one for sentimental things, are we?"

"I don't have a lot that I want to remember."

He looked her in the eye. "Maybe that will change."

They stared at each other, the words hanging heavy in the air. It was a promise that took two people. Did she want it? Or not?

Grace turned away, heading towards the living room. "Thanks for your help today. I'm sure you're tired. I know I am."

He scooped up his laptop and wine, following behind her. She grabbed a book, tucking her legs under her as she settled into an armchair.

Hunter knew she'd read until she fell asleep. She had done it every night they'd been together and every night since he had been in Darling. But just because Grace was predictable didn't mean that he knew her anymore.

Old Grace wouldn't have minded if Hunter had joined her in the living room. New Grace just might neuter him. "Mind if I hang out?"

She kept her gaze on her book. "I don't mind."

Not exactly an enthusiastic response, but beggars couldn't be choosers. Hunter balanced his laptop in one hand and the wineglass in the other as he settled onto the couch.

He clicked back through the photos, enjoying the forest all over again as he relived it in his pictures. It was hard to believe he had already been in Darling for a week.

What was harder to believe was that he didn't want to leave. Some people hated change. But Hunter hated when things stayed the same. Except he was finally realizing that all that adventure didn't mean a damn thing if he didn't have someone to share it with.

Not just someone. Grace.

If that meant being in Darling, then that's where he wanted to be.

He was halfway through his glass of wine when it hit him. Hunter hadn't thought about Jack once today.

Hunter felt two inches tall, enjoying life while his best friend was gone. He wasn't to blame for what happened to Jack. But would Hunter ever stop feeling guilty about not spending more time with his friend when he had the chance?

His eyes burned. That was exactly why he couldn't give up on him and Grace. He had enough regrets. He didn't want the love of his life to be another one.

"You okay?" Grace asked.

Hunter blinked, coming back to reality. "Yeah. Sorry. Zoned out."

"You looked like you were about to cry."

"No, it's just—" His voice cracked.

"Jack." She looked at him with so much compassion he

just about burst into tears. "You're in luck. I'm a good listener. So is Ruby."

He chewed the inside of his cheek. How could he put into words the hole that was ripped open inside him? A gaping, painful place where it seemed all the goodness in life had drained from his body? "I should be over it by now."

Grace closed her book. "Should you? It's only been two weeks, Hunter. And I've always kind of thought the saying that time heals all wounds is a load of crap."

"Really? You seem to be doing well two years later."

"That's what you think." Grace picked up her glass with a wink. "If you stick around any longer, I'm going to need a wine fridge."

He blew air through his lips. "Sorry. I didn't mean to drag you down with me. Pathetic, huh?"

"Not at all. Why do you think romance books and movies and songs are so popular? Because everyone is looking to feel something. So many people go their entire lives without knowing their own heart. So even though I can't imagine how much losing Jack hurt, I think there is something beautiful that you can feel so deeply. That you loved him so much."

"Are we talking about Jack anymore?"

"Yes, we're talking about Jack. Anything else is ancient history." Her voice was flat.

He stiffened. If their relationship was firmly in the past, then why did it bother him so much? "Ancient history, huh?"

"Yep. Don't you remember taking photos for my dating profile today? I've moved on, Hunter. I told you that, but you're just living in your own world as usual. Still trying to carry out your grand plan, no matter how crazy it is."

His chest grew tight. This hadn't always been the grand plan.

No, the grand plan was to forget about Grace. Grieve

Jack. Leave here. Divorce Grace. Return to real life and never look back. The grand plan was sure as hell not to care about anyone this much again. Look where that had gotten him. The three most important people in his life were gone.

That pretty much left Dana, a fact that would have her rolling on the floor in laughter. While Dana was like family, she wasn't exactly the warm and fuzzy type. "I'm just feeling melancholy, I guess. Maybe red wine isn't my drink."

"I get it. You're not in a good place right now. You'll feel better when you get back to work."

Another reminder that, in her eyes, this was temporary. But he wouldn't give up. Not yet.

He forced a smile and grabbed his laptop. "You're right."

"And Hunter?"

"What's that?"

She looked him in the eye. "Time doesn't heal all wounds. But it does help you forget."

He held her gaze, searching for answers. Forget what? That she loved him? Or forget how much he had hurt her? He supposed the difference didn't matter. What mattered was making this right.

Grace spent her time reading love stories. Hunter wanted her to live one.

CHAPTER THIRTEEN

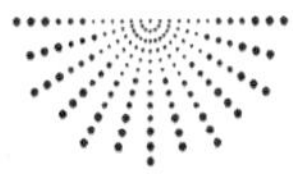

GRACE

Grace shoved her phone into the drawer under the cash register. Hunter wouldn't be back from the Buck for a couple of hours at least. Once he got into his work trance, it was hard to tell when he would come out of it. But better to be safe than sorry.

It was dumb enough that she spent all day looking at the picture of the two of them. Even worse would be if someone caught her doing it, especially Hunter himself.

She wasn't delusional. Hunter didn't really want to rekindle things. He wasn't thinking right after losing Jack. He was hurting and looking for comfort. Grace had provided him with a place to stay. That was as much comfort as she was willing to offer.

But Grace could sense him reaching for her, seeking the emotional support that came with a relationship. Well, tough. He couldn't divorce his cake and eat it too.

Not that Hunter could know how hard it was for her to keep her distance. He probably thought she was heartless. If only he knew that it took all her willpower not to lose herself in him again. But the only thing harder than not getting pulled in again would be caring too much, only to be tossed to the side when work called his name.

No, thank you. She had lived that story once before. Once had been quite enough.

The bell over the door chimed as Vivian stepped inside the coffee shop. Except this time, she wasn't dropping off pastries. "Your fairy godmother is here."

"I should be playing your fairy godmother. I'm way older than you."

"We could pass for sisters." Vivian handed Grace the canvas bag. "This was everything I have. It's not much."

"As long as it's not jeans and a T-shirt, then it's better than anything I have." Grace peeked inside the bag.

"Are you sure you don't want to ask Elle? She's the stylish one."

"No way. The last thing I want is for the entire town to know about this."

Vivian tilted her head. "But you're going to the Buck. Kind of defeats the goal of discretion."

Grace sighed. Vivian had a point. But what options did Grace have? The Buck was the only place in town to go on a date.

Matt was coming to Darling so that they could finally meet in person after chatting for a week. Grace had offered to go to Juneau, but he insisted on being the one to travel. It was really nice of him. If only she weren't nervous enough to hurl. Even though Grace didn't plan on getting in a serious relationship ever again, she was still anxious about going on a first date for the first time in two decades. "Maybe I should cancel."

"Then you better do it fast. He's probably got one foot on the ferry by now."

Grace bit her lip. "So you think I should cancel?"

Vivian barked a laugh. "Heck no. This guy is mildly attractive and not crazy? This is Alaska, and you just struck gold. I think you should hold on to him with both hands. Besides, you said you wanted to go on a date by your fortieth birthday. Here's your chance."

Grace shifted to her other foot. So much for getting out of it. "Just seems like a big inconvenience for him. Then he has to spend the night. An entire day is a lot of time to devote to just a dinner date."

"This wouldn't have anything to do with a certain handsome photographer living upstairs, would it?"

Grace looked everywhere but at Vivian. "What? No! Divorced, remember? Or almost divorced."

She had explained the situation to Vivian, leaving out the part where Hunter was convinced that he and Grace belonged together. Why complicate things unnecessarily? It wasn't like they were going to rekindle things, despite what Hunter thought. Not with just twenty-four days left to sort out almost twenty years of history between them.

"If you say so. Do you need anything else? Want help getting ready?"

Grace shook her head. "You've already gone above and beyond the call of duty. I think I've got it from here."

Vivian smiled over her shoulder as she stepped outside. "Good luck. Not that you need it. You're a catch."

Grace's stomach knotted up. If only. Vivian was just being nice. But Grace would take what she could get. After so many years of not staying in one place long enough to get to know people, Vivian was the closest friend Grace had had in years.

The bell chimed again as someone else came into the coffee shop. Grace shoved the bag in a cabinet and got to work. The rest of the day, she was too busy frothing milk and pulling shots of espresso to do anything else to get ready for her date. If only her stomach would stop jumping around.

She was excited about the date. Not nervous. Excited.

Finally, Grace flicked off the *Open* sign and rushed through her cleaning routine.

She lifted the apron over her head and hung it on the hook behind the counter. Grace took a deep breath. She had a date to get ready for. Preferably when Hunter wasn't around to give her a hard time.

Grace had just grabbed the bag of clothes when the door opened, and Hunter walked in. Her shoulders sagged. Dammit. So much for getting ready for her date without him around. No way he'd let her live this down.

Ruby jumped up from her bed and trotted over to greet him. Grace sighed. Not even the dog was immune to his charms.

Hunter gathered Ruby in his arms, smiling at Grace. "Ready?"

Grace eyed him. "Ready for what?"

"Your transformation, Cinderella. You think I'd forget about your date? It's the most exciting thing in my life right now."

"That's sad."

"That's Alaska." He winked. "Now, come on. Let's get you ready."

"I do love a good makeover scene," Grace agreed as they headed upstairs. "But why do I need a transformation? You always told me I was a natural beauty."

"Ah, well. I am the exception. Most men are idiots. We have to prepare for the worst."

She chewed on her lip. That was exactly her problem. Hunter was the exception, which was probably why moving on had taken so damn long.

Once they were upstairs, Hunter set his backpack aside and pointed at the canvas bag. "What have we got there?"

Grace handed it to him, and he pulled out the three dresses Vivian had brought over.

His eyes twinkled. "You know what this means, right? Fashion show."

"Only because I have to try them on anyway." She took the dresses back from him and went into her room to change.

The first dress was too short. She didn't even bother to show Hunter. There was no way she was wearing that one. Grace was self-conscious about her height as it was.

The second dress was so tight that his eyes nearly popped out of his head when he saw it. "No imagination needed."

Grace laughed. "Hopefully, the third time's the charm. Otherwise, I'm going to show up in jeans in a sweatshirt."

"In that case, let's hope he has a lot of imagination."

The last one was a navy blue maxi dress. Or maybe it was a maxi dress on Vivian. It was practically knee-length on Grace. She flapped her arms. "The flowy sleeves hide my old lady arms."

"Don't you dare say that. I've seen your guns behind the espresso machine."

She turned in front of him. "You really like it? This won't scare him off?"

His eyes softened. "If it does, then good riddance. The man has no taste at all. Now, what's the plan for hair and makeup?"

Grace massaged her forehead. Crap. She hadn't even thought about that. If things didn't work out with Matt, she was deleting the app. Dating was too much damn work, especially when she liked being alone. Most of the time. "I don't know. Nothing?"

"I am pretty sure I spotted a makeup bag in the bathroom."

"It's an artifact. Haven't used it since I've been here."

"Then allow me."

Grace raised an eyebrow. "What do you know about makeup?"

Hunter splayed his hand against his chest. "Excuse me. I am an artist. I have a great eye, if you remember."

"I remember you have a great ego," she grumbled, following him to the bathroom.

He laid out the contents of the makeup bag on the counter, inspecting each one. Hunter sharpened the eyeliner and tested the lipstick on his wrist. "We're in luck. It still has slightly more moisture than the Sahara."

Despite her nerves, Grace couldn't help but smile. She and Hunter had actually been to the Sahara once on assignment. How was she supposed to get over her ex when the entire world held memories of their time together?

Of course, it didn't help that he was right in front of her face. Literally.

Hunter didn't even blink as he flicked on eyeliner and dabbed on lipstick. Grace had always been in awe of his concentration. And right now, he was looking at her the way he did when he was lost in a photo.

Not that she was that conceited.

Before she could stop herself, her memories took her back to when they were in the Daintree, the oldest tropical rainforest in the world. Hunter had been as excited as a little kid as they walked through it. So excited that he had accidentally let a branch loose too soon, whipping Grace in the face.

Grace had let out a choice word, and Hunter had been by her side in a minute.

She had reached up to touch her cheek and then had looked down at her hands. Red had smeared her fingertips.

"Here," Hunter had said. "Let me help."

He had used his water bottle and a bandana to clean the cut. After wiping at it with an antiseptic wipe, he had dotted on liquid bandage. "That'll have to last until we get out of here. Look on the bright side. If it scars, you'll have a cool story to tell."

"Victim of a tree? Doesn't sound very cool." Grace had frowned. "Do you really think it'll scar?"

"Why?" Hunter had teased. "Thinking about getting back on the dating market?"

Grace had stuck her tongue out of him. Of course she wasn't. The idea of being with anyone besides Hunter was so crazy that her brain couldn't even comprehend it. She couldn't imagine loving another person as much as him. Not ever.

"You've always been the most beautiful woman in the world. Nothing is going to change that." Hunter had leaned in to kiss her, and they had almost done it in the rainforest. Grace could still remember the smell of the damp earth, the surrounding sounds.

The scratch hadn't scarred in the end. For the longest time, Grace had been disappointed about that. She had wanted to carry every memory of Hunter with her forever. The irony being that it had left a scar, just one invisible to the outside world. A moment in time that her heart refused to purge even all these years later.

Hunter cleared his throat, bringing her back to this moment. "Thinking about the Daintree?"

"How did you know?"

"I was thinking about it too."

He was so close to her right now. Close enough to kiss.

Her breath hitched. Where the hell had that come from? She needed to get away from him before she did something stupid. "All done?"

Hunter nodded, placing his hands on her shoulders and turning her towards the mirror. "What do you think?"

Grace let out a gasp, reaching up to touch her cheek. He had highlighted her brown eyes, making them luminous. Her lips were a rosy color, breathing life into her face. She looked radiant. Vivian had some serious competition for the role of fairy godmother. "Seriously. Are you moonlighting as a makeup artist or something?"

He chuckled. "Like I said, I have a good eye. I've always been able to see things that others can't."

Grace took a deep breath, trying to ignore the fact that her heart rate had doubled. He was talking about his photography. No need to get her engine roaring over that. "So, what are you going to do tonight?"

"Well, considering the only thing to do in town is go to the Buck, and you probably don't want me there, I'm thinking hang out here? Maybe go for a walk? It's practically light out all night anyway."

"Take Ruby if you go, will you? I feel guilty leaving her home."

"You don't need to feel guilty."

Grace searched his eyes. Guilty for what? But she didn't ask. This was always how it had been with Hunter. Saying something without saying anything at all. "Okay, then I won't feel guilty. I'm too busy feeling nervous."

Hunter looked up at the ceiling. "Dear God, you're high-maintenance."

"Am not," she snapped.

"Whatever you say." Hunter held up his hands. "Can I get you a glass of wine or something? Maybe an anti-anxiety prescription?"

Grace glanced at her smartwatch. She didn't have the time, but she didn't want to start her date feeling like a jumbled-up mess either. "A glass of wine wouldn't be so bad. A small one."

"You got it. You drink, and I'll give you a pep talk." Hunter ducked into the kitchen and came back with a wineglass for her. "You have no reason to be nervous. This guy is probably just happy there's a woman in Alaska to date, okay?"

"Hey. I was promised a pep talk, not the truth."

"The truth is you look great, and if he's too stupid to see that, then that's his problem."

Grace took a gulp of her wine. Rich words coming from a man guilty of exactly that. Finishing the glass in record time, she handed it back to him.

She hesitated. Should she hug him goodbye? Kiss him on the cheek? No, that was actually insane. There was another guy waiting for her at the Buck right now. So why did she feel so weird about leaving Hunter? "Thanks for your help."

Grace grabbed her purse and slammed the door behind her, hurrying across the street to the Buck. She needed to get the hell away from Hunter.

Sure, he was attractive. Hunter had always been good-looking. And Grace would be lying if she said the thought of being with him again hadn't crossed her mind.

But Grace wasn't interested. They were just familiar with each other, that was all. And the physical attraction? A result of conditioning and deprivation. The perfect storm.

Grace squared her shoulders and stepped into the restaurant, searching the room for her date. Hunter wasn't the guy she should be thinking about right now.

Or ever.

She gulped. So much for not being a jumbled-up mess.

CHAPTER FOURTEEN

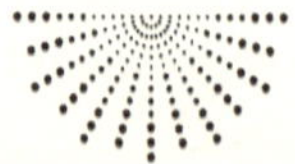

HUNTER

Hunter checked his watch. Twenty-five minutes.

It took all his willpower not to peek out the front window of the apartment over the coffee shop and see if he could spot Grace and her date at the Buck. But the least Hunter could do was give her privacy for a few hours. That's all the time it would take for her to realize that she didn't like the bozo, or any bozos, except for Hunter. He was sure of it.

But was it his fault that time had stopped?

As if peeping out the window wasn't bad enough, he briefly considered walking by the front of the Buck. Not that there was anything wrong with an innocent stroll down Main Street.

With a sigh, Hunter rested his head against the back of the couch. He hated feeling this way—helpless and, worse, jealous. Grace had wanted to date again, and he had offered to help. That was part of the deal. Part of the deal was also that he could date too. But there was only one woman he wanted to be with, and she was across the street with another man.

Hunter pushed himself up from the couch. He was getting dangerously close to a pity party. No good ever came from that. He needed a distraction.

He wandered into the kitchen, grabbing the peanut butter and jelly from the fridge. It was well past dinnertime, and Hunter had never been much of a cook. After he fixed himself a sandwich, Hunter cleaned up the dirty dishes and wiped down the counters. He might be a mess, but he didn't want to leave the kitchen in the same state.

Carrying his plate to the table, Hunter stared at the food, his stomach churning. He forced himself to take a few bites before pushing the plate away.

Hunter glanced at his watch again. Forty-seven minutes.

He wrapped up the rest of the sandwich for later and grabbed a beer from the fridge instead.

Hunter winced at the first sip, the bitter brew a sharp contrast to the sweet jelly. The second sip went down easier.

He paced the living room, and Ruby followed his movements with her crystal-blue eyes.

Hunter tried to reason with himself. He and Grace had history. Complicated history. Even though he still wasn't exactly sure what made Grace walk away, it was clear she hadn't forgiven him yet.

But Hunter enjoyed being with her. He liked sharing the small apartment with her. He couldn't stop thinking about the damn woman.

She was just as amazing now as the day they had met. Grace was kind and smart and independent. She didn't fawn over him like every person he crossed paths with these days, and she never had. Grace treated him like an equal and expected the same treatment in return.

Not to mention, she was beautiful.

His heart squeezed. But just because Hunter wasn't over Grace didn't mean she wasn't over him. After all, she was on a date. With someone who wasn't Hunter.

He cracked his neck. Why hadn't he listened to Jack when he and Grace had first split up? But there was no changing the past. The best Hunter could do was to not lose sight of what mattered again.

That wasn't his only problem. Grace hadn't been wrong when she pointed out that, eventually, he would have to leave for work. Dana could help him delay things for a while. But forever?

Not to mention that Hunter had built his life on change and excitement and variety. But he would give it all up for Grace in a heartbeat. He'd throw his exciting life away if it meant a life with her in it.

Hunter took a swig of his beer. Time wasn't on his side. The divorce would be finalized in a little more than three weeks. It wasn't enough time. It wasn't enough to make up for years of mistakes. It wasn't enough to know for sure if she still felt about him the way he did about her. It wasn't enough to be certain that if he did give his career up, there was something worth giving it up for.

But it was more time than Jack had.

Besides, Hunter had always put his work first, as Grace had pointed out more than once. He had made choices for his career that had paid off, and some of those choices included sacrifice.

And why wouldn't he have? He had seen his Aunt Linda try to fit in, a square peg in a round hole. She stuck out life in the small western town for Hunter's sake, and he would always be grateful for that. But Hunter wasn't that strong. He was selfish and weak. Things hadn't ended well with Grace before. What if the same thing happened this time, despite his best intentions?

In his line of work, personal relationships weren't a priority at best, and they were a hindrance at worst. Some would say it wasn't worth it.

His life was a one-in-a-million chance, the grand prize in a cereal box. If that meant he died lonely and rich with a lifetime of adventures, then many would consider him to have lived a better life than most.

Not too long ago, he would have been one of those people. But after what happened with Jack, Hunter didn't see things the same way anymore. After all, what did any of that matter if he wasn't able to share his life, incredible or not, with the one he loved?

He finished his beer and checked his watch again. One hour, two minutes. Hunter debated cracking open another bottle, but he needed to slow down. Otherwise, Grace would have to scrape him off the floor by the time she got home.

His chest grew tight as the room seemed to close in around him. The apartment quickly went from cozy to claustrophobic. Sitting here stewing was doing him no good. Too bad he couldn't do what he really wanted, which was to storm over to the restaurant and interrogate Grace's date.

Hunter clapped his hands together. "Come on, Ruby. Let's go for that walk I promised."

The dog pranced to the door. Hunter clipped on her leash and led them outside. He headed around the back of the building and away from Main Street and the Buck, avoiding temptation. This way, he wouldn't gawk at Grace like she was a goldfish in an aquarium. Seeing her with another man definitely wouldn't do Hunter's emotions any good. And if she saw Hunter, it would go over like a lead balloon. He was trying to prove to her that dating sucked, not that he sucked.

Hunter zipped up his jacket. Even though it was still light outside, the island grew colder as the day grew later. It almost felt like a different season from just a few hours ago.

The low cloud cover turned Darling gray, making it look like a scene from a noir film.

He kept walking away from town, not exactly sure where he was heading. Hunter hoped that if Grace was out of sight, she would be out of mind. It was a futile task, considering that she had been out of sight for two years, but his heart still hadn't forgotten her.

Not to mention the frustration of trying to distract himself in the one place on Earth that didn't have any distractions. Next time he was in a situation like this—which he hoped to God would be never—it better be in New York City or London or Rio. Sure as hell not in the quietest place on the planet.

He went down to the waterfront, following it out of town. That would make it easy to find his way back. Going for a walk in the dark wasn't his best idea ever, but it was a better way to kill time than getting drunk.

Ruby was a good sport, prancing alongside Hunter happily. At least one of them was having a good night.

Hunter glanced up at the sky. As dusk fell over the island, the light continued to change. He should've brought his camera. It was a testimony to his state of mind that he hadn't even thought of it. His equipment was part of his body. It felt like something was missing when he didn't have it.

His feet grew heavy at the reminder of everything he would give up if he stayed here with Grace. Did she even realize what he was willing to sacrifice? It would be giving up who he was.

Isn't that what you asked Grace to do all those years?

His throat grew tight. Pretty much. Hunter had always blamed Grace for her unhappiness. She knew what she was getting into when they got married. Looking back, he saw how stupid that had been. Yeah, she knew what she was getting into. But he hadn't. He had been too damn selfish to understand how much compromise a successful relationship took.

As they reached the edge of town, the trees grew thicker. It was quiet out here, just the gently falling rain and the sound of the waves lapping against the shore. Hunter could almost hear himself think.

He found a stump and took a seat, letting out the leash so Ruby could sniff around.

Trying not to feel ridiculous, Hunter closed his eyes and attempted to focus on nothing in particular. Not Jack, not Grace, and not what the hell he was doing with his life.

Jack had been a fan of meditation, always encouraging Hunter to try it. He never had, of course. The last thing Hunter had wanted to do was sit still when there was the whole world to see. It was something else Hunter regretted not making time for when his best friend was still around. But there was no time like the present. Maybe it would help clear his mind. If nothing else, it was a connection to Jack. Perhaps he had more wisdom to share with Hunter, now that he was finally listening. If Jack wasn't too busy laughing at him.

A branch snapped, startling Hunter. His eyes flew open. Sitting in the forest with his eyes closed had been an idiot move. Darling may not have much crime, but there were wild animals to think about. Hunter had enough up-close encounters in his lifetime to know to respect wildlife.

Heart pounding, he scanned the area where the noise had come from. The branches rustled, and he tensed, ready to run. He didn't think he could outrun a bear, but he had jack-all to defend himself. Running was his only option. He gathered Ruby up, prepared to carry her to safety with him.

Before he could make a move, the branches parted, and he found himself face-to-face with an older woman. She wore a long rain jacket, a few wisps of fine hair escaping from under her hood.

She blinked at him. "Oh. Sorry to disturb you. I almost never see other people on these little walks of mine."

Hunter's heart rate slowed down a smidge. Not a bear. For the second time in the last five seconds, he felt like an idiot. "I'm Hunter."

"I know." She smiled. "I'm Natasha. Nice to meet you."

Hunter smiled back briefly, his mind racing. How did she know who he was? They had definitely never met before. Maybe Natasha knew him from online, even though she didn't look like the social media type. "Well, I won't bother you on your walks again. I'm just visiting."

"Are you? I was hoping you would stay."

He shifted on the stump. Not just an old woman. A crazy old woman. What did it matter to her if he stayed in Darling or not? "Do you need help getting back to town? You're not out here alone, are you?"

"I'm never alone." Natasha looked up at the sky. "But I think it's time for you to be heading back now, don't you?"

The hair on the back of his neck stood up. Little old lady or not, something about her gave him the creeps. He almost would've preferred a wild animal. He set Ruby on the ground and stood. "Probably. Have a good night."

She waved as he walked away.

Hunter figured it was still too early for Grace to be home, but he wasn't in the mood to hang out with spooky old ladies in the forest. So much for a relaxing walk.

Ruby flopped down on her dog bed the minute they got home.

Hunter scratched her ears. "You wouldn't do too good on one of my work trips, you know that? I'd have to carry you in a backpack."

His phone buzzed in his pocket, and he reached for it. Probably Dana. She was the only one who ever called him.

His eyebrows climbed up his forehead when he saw the caller ID. He had exchanged numbers with Wolfie his first few days working at the Buck. Hunter enjoyed chatting with the older man, and if he did stick around Darling, it would be nice to have a friend. But Wolfie had never called him before. Why would he when they saw each other almost every day? "Hey, Wolfie, what's going on?"

Wolfie blew air into the phone. "It's Grace's date. I keep swinging by their table to keep an eye on things. Twice, I have heard her say she's ready to go home, and this guy lays on the guilt to get her to stay. I wanted to give you the first chance to set him straight. Otherwise, I'm going to step in."

Hunter set his jaw. He wasn't confused anymore. Now he was pissed. "I'll be right there."

He ended the call and stormed across the street, flinging open the door to the Buck. A breeze slammed it shut behind him, and every head in the place turned his way. But Hunter was only focused on one person.

Taking a deep breath, he walked over to the booth with the slow, controlled steps of someone who knew exactly what he was doing.

Kicking some accountant ass.

Grace's eyes widened. "Hunter. What are you doing here?"

"Who is this?" the man across from her asked. He smiled, but his tone told Hunter to get lost.

"This is Hunter, my ex—"

"Husband." Hunter glared at the man. "I'm her husband."

Matt looked at Grace. "I thought you were divorced."

She gave a feeble shrug. "It's a work in progress. We've been separated for two years."

Hunter placed his hands on the table and leaned forward.

He was going to make sure this guy heard the message loud and clear. "The thing is, I had to make sure she didn't end up with an asshole. And I hear you're an asshole. So this just isn't going to work."

Matt reached across the table, covering Grace's hand with his. She paled slightly. "Our date has nothing to do with you."

"Wrong answer. The date is over."

Matt laughed. "You're joking, right?"

"Why don't we take this outside and see if I'm in a joking mood?"

"This really isn't necessary—" Grace tried to argue, but the two men were already heading for the front door.

By the time they made it out to Main Street, faces crowded every window of the Buck. Matt stood across from him, clenching his fists. There wasn't a car in sight, and Hunter half expected a tumbleweed to blow down the street.

A laugh bubbled up inside him. How the hell had he ended up in a Wild West shootout? All he knew was that this guy wasn't good enough for Grace. No man ever would be. Maybe not even Hunter himself. But dammit if he wouldn't try. "Just so we're clear, you better never talk to Grace again. Or come back to town. She deserves better."

"Says the guy she is divorcing," Matt sneered.

"Please, stop." Grace burst out of the doors of the Buck, and Hunter turned to look at her. "This is ridiculous. Fighting is so stupid—"

Before she could finish, before Hunter could even look back at Matt, something whacked him on the head. Hard.

With a grunt, Hunter fell to the ground, his eyes fluttering closed. The last thing he saw before blacking out was Grace punching Matt square in the nose.

Hunter smiled as the world drifted away.

That was his girl.

CHAPTER FIFTEEN

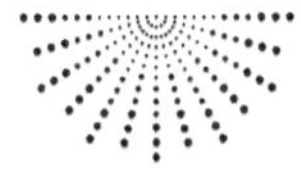

GRACE

"Hunter." Grace shook his arm. "Hunter, wake up."

Panic clawed at her chest. Oh God. What if he didn't? Darling didn't even have a doctor.

"Let me see." Wolfie squatted down next to her. He checked Hunter's pulse first, then listened to his breathing. "He's okay. Just give him a minute."

Grace's eyes burned. She had been dreading this date, and now look what had happened. The guy had been a complete jerk, and Hunter was unconscious in the middle of Main Street.

Her breath hitched. But he had been there for her.

A groan came from the ground, and her heart leapt into her throat. "Hunter?"

He blinked his eyes open, his gaze settling on her. "So much for rescuing you. Where did you learn to throw a punch like that?"

With a trembling hand, she wiped at her nose. Good question. It was like she had become possessed the minute

Matt hit Hunter. "I have no idea. I guess I was my own knight in shining armor."

"Apparently, you were mine too." Hunter turned his head to the side. "Where's the asshole?"

Her throat tightened. Hunter was lying on the ground, covered in gravel and dirt, and she had felt a lump on his head when she was checking him over. But the first thing he thought about was taking care of Grace.

"The asshole has left," Wolfie said. "Or at least fled to his room at the lodge. I think he'll be on the first ferry out of here in the morning."

Hunter smiled at Grace. "Must be afraid of you. I sure as hell am."

She shook her head as she helped him up, brushing off his back.

Wolfie gestured to the restaurant. "You two want to come back in for a bit? There's a table with your name on it." He gave Hunter a pointed look. "Although you probably shouldn't drink, just to be on the safe side. You took a pretty good hit to the head."

Hunter looked at Grace. "Only if you want to. I can be your sober walker."

She swallowed. Damn him. Just when she was getting over Hunter, he had to become everything she ever wanted.

Or maybe he always has been.

Grace took a shaky breath. There was only one way to find out. She couldn't write them off just yet. "I had hoped for a fun night. I don't see why one bad moment should change that."

Hunter offered her his arm, and they followed Wolfie back inside.

Instead of going to the booth, Hunter led her towards the bar.

Grace dug her fingers into his arm. "Wolfie was right. You shouldn't drink."

"I agree. But if I were in your shoes, I'd be thirsty right now."

She barked a laugh. Between her disaster of a date, the fight on Main Street, and the relief that Hunter actually seemed okay after getting knocked in the head, a drink didn't sound like a bad idea. "Why not?"

Hunter rested an elbow on the bar. "What are you in the mood for? Beer? Wine?"

Grace squinted as she scanned the colorful bottles. "Tequila."

He let out a whistle. "Pulling out all the stops."

"It's not often a lady gets to defend her own honor."

Wolfie poured a shot for Grace, handing her the saltshaker and a lime wedge. He served Hunter a glass of water.

Grace clinked her tequila to Hunter's water. "To being single forever."

The amber liquid burned her throat, leaving a trail of warmth as it traveled through her body.

Grace sucked on the lime wedge, smacking her lips. "Next time I get the wild hair to go on a date, remind me to do a tequila shot instead. It's much more satisfying."

Hunter chuckled. "What the hell happened? Must've been one crappy date."

Grace set down the empty shot glass. She was still trying to figure out that part herself, and she didn't like the conclusion she kept arriving at. "As much as it pains me to say this, I think you were right. He said whatever he needed to say online. Once he got here, that much was obvious. Not to mention, he thought that if he came all the way here, I would go back with him to his room tonight."

"Men suck. Have I told you that before?"

"Trust me. I've learned the hard way."

"Let me make it up to you. You're all dressed up. It's Saturday night. We're already at the restaurant." He bobbed his head in the direction of the empty booth where Grace and Matt had sat earlier. "What do you think? Go on a date with me?"

Grace eyed the empty shot glass, suddenly thirsty for a second drink. Hunter sent her emotions into a tailspin on a good day, let alone when she was already rattled. But they had already made fools of themselves. What did she have to lose?

Maybe you have everything to gain.

She bit the inside of her cheek. Wasn't the point of the dating app to prove she was over Hunter? Not fall for him again? "Have you eaten yet?"

"Half of a PB&J." He held up a finger. "And before you ask, I did take Ruby for a walk. But please know it took everything I had not to case the Buck while I was at it."

Grace fought a smile. Did Hunter have any idea how irresistible that made him? It was one thing to do what he said he would. It was another for him to take care of Ruby. "Fine. But only because I don't want you complaining that you're hungry later. And for the record, this is not a date. It's just dinner."

They made their way over to the booth, where Wolfie met up with them and promptly took their order.

Grace's stomach growled when he brought out the vegetarian pizza, along with a beer for her. She had been so anxious on her date with Matt that she hadn't been able to eat more than a few bites. The artichoke hearts and sun-dried tomatoes on a sourdough crust tasted like heaven.

After she finished her third slice, Grace took a sip of her beer and set her phone on the table. She pulled up the dating app and deleted her profile.

Hunter arched an eyebrow. "Pretty serious about staying single forever, huh?"

"For the rest of my life. I gave it the good old college try. Dating. Marriage. All of it. I'm just not meant to be one-half of a pair."

He set down his half-eaten slice. "You can't really think that. You're not the problem, Grace. I am. I let you down."

She shifted in her seat. His words tugged on her heartstrings, and she didn't like it. After spending the last two years telling herself she didn't care about Hunter, Grace was realizing nothing could be further from the truth. But she had to lie to him, and to herself, to keep from getting lost in Hunter again. At least until she was certain of her feelings and his. "Don't worry about it. I'm happy here."

For the most part, she was. Sure, moving to Alaska hadn't been the grand plan. But Grace had what she wanted, right? She had a home and Ruby. She ran her own business. She liked the people in Darling, and the feeling seemed to be mutual.

If only Hunter hadn't crashed back into her life and made her realize how much more fun it was to be here with him. How much more fun everything was when they were together.

Sitting across from that jerk tonight, Grace had wished it was Hunter she was having dinner with. When he had shown up, Grace had been both relieved and upset. It worried her how happy she was to see him.

Not that she could tell Hunter any of this. He might be convinced they belonged together, but Grace remembered very clearly all the reasons they did not.

Well, mostly. The level of clarity depended on the presence of the dimple.

His gray eyes turned down. "What happened, Grace?

What made you happy here that didn't make you happy with me? What did I do?"

She took a swig of her beer, wishing it would drown every single feeling inside her. Because the truth was that it wasn't just one thing. It was years of her soul being chipped away at, of losing herself in Hunter piece by piece. Then, it only took one single moment when Grace wasn't strong enough to be with him anymore, and she cracked. She had nothing left to lose because she was already completely lost. "It doesn't matter, Hunter. That time, us, it's in the past. We just need to focus on right now."

He stood from the table so suddenly that her beer sloshed in the glass. "I need a minute."

Grace's gaze followed him as he walked away, disappointment heavy in her stomach. Apparently, he was done with the conversation. Not that she should be surprised. Hunter had always been better at going than staying.

But he headed in the opposite direction of the door. Hunter wove his way through the room, punching buttons on the jukebox.

Grace scrunched her forehead. What the hell was he doing? Mood music? It was just like him to avoid having a real conversation. Hunter never took anything seriously.

Then the song changed, and her train of thought came to a screeching halt.

He hadn't put on just any music. It was their song.

Hunter walked back to the booth and offered her his hand. "Here is the truth. I've done a lot of shitty things in my life. But I never once stopped loving you with my whole heart. Now, will you please dance with me so I can show the world how damn special you are?"

Her heart slammed into her ribs. She wanted to tell him he was being ridiculous. That he was wasting his time, their time, because they both knew how the story ended. That

Hunter could not possibly be her hero, because the hero made everything better, not more confusing.

But something about the tone of his voice and the look in his eyes told her heart everything she needed to know. Maybe things could be different this time. Maybe they did belong together. Because the truth was that after all these years, she hadn't stopped loving him either. "But dancing is on Friday nights."

He quirked up the corner of his mouth. "That's what you got out of all that? I'm not waiting until Friday to dance with my wife. Are you going to give me a chance to be your Prince Charming or not? I already missed the opportunity to be your knight in shining armor, thanks to your killer right hook."

Her head spun. Grace looked from Hunter to the dance floor to her glass. Oh, what the hell?

Grace gulped the last of her beer and placed her hand in his, her body warming at his touch. Based on the way his gray eyes darkened to the color of a stormy sky, she guessed he felt it too.

She took a deep breath as she faced him. She had kept her distance from Hunter. She had been determined to stay mad at him. He had come here to process his grief, not to rekindle things between them.

But all those good intentions flew out the window as she remembered just how damn good it felt to be with him. It had taken less than two weeks of being with Hunter to undo her, thread by thread.

She shuffled her feet, painfully aware that every gaze in the Buck was on them. "We're really giving these people a show tonight, huh? They're going to be sad to see you go. You're the most exciting thing in this town since who knows how long."

"Unless I don't go."

"Don't joke, Hunter."

"What do you want? Do you want me to stay?"

Her chest tightened. Now he wanted to know what she wanted? After all those years of following him around and doing what he wanted?

It would be stupid to ask him to stay. The stupidest thing she'd ever done. After two years of hating Hunter, she was about to be divorced. Free. And now, with just a little more than three weeks to go, he offered her the world on a silver platter. "Things can never be simple with you, huh? Do you sit up at night and think about new ways to torture me?"

Hunter wielded his dimple like a magic wand. "You got one thing right. I sit up at night and think about you. How much I miss you. How much I want you."

The room suddenly felt too hot, but she couldn't blame it on the alcohol. Oh no, that wasn't why her body was betraying her. It was because she wanted Hunter too.

"Grace Hart. Are you blushing?"

"No," she stammered, looking away. "Don't look so goddamn pleased with yourself. It's your fault. Stupid dimple."

"I'm willing to take the blame." Hunter leaned forward and whispered in her ear. "Want to get out of here?"

Her stomach did a flip-flop. Grace glanced around to make sure no one could overhear them. "I'm not looking for a one-night stand."

"Collectively, it wouldn't be."

Well. Wasn't that the truth? Only Hunter could be familiar and exciting at the same time. "Let's go."

With a grin, Hunter slapped a few bills on the table and led Grace out of the Buck.

She tried to think straight as they headed across the street. It was the end of a long day. She had been emotional. She had done a tequila shot. Grace shouldn't want Hunter, this man she'd loved and left once, to get closer to her. But she had never wanted anything so badly. The minute the door closed behind them, she kicked logic to the curb.

Grace grabbed the collar of his shirt and pressed her lips to his.

Hunter broke away with a gasp, his gray eyes searching hers. "You sure?

A wave of fire passed through her body at the husky tone in his voice. "Yes."

"God, I missed you." Hunter pulled her close and kissed her until her toes curled.

They fumbled their way through the apartment. Ruby lifted her head briefly as they passed by the dog bed in the living room. Once in Grace's bedroom, she closed the door behind them.

Hunter flicked on the light, and she crossed her arms over her chest, even though she was still fully dressed.

"Cold feet?" Hunter asked.

"Shy feet."

His lips twitched. "Grace. We were married for fifteen years. The time to be shy has passed."

"But I'm older now. And it's been two years."

He moved closer, purring in her ear. "Two years to crave you, my love. Two years to miss every inch of your body. Two years to miss everything about you."

She licked her lips. "When you put it that way."

"How about I go first?" He pulled off his shirt, his abs rippling with each movement.

Lust clawed at her, and she pounced on him. "Damn you."

With a laugh, he discarded her clothes one by one and lowered her to the bed. "My God, you're beautiful," he whispered, doing everything right.

It was exactly like she remembered and somehow better than before. Grace couldn't remember a time before Hunter nor imagine a time after him. For the first time since parting ways with Hunter, life seemed exciting again. She felt completely alive.

They lay in bed together, her head resting on his chest. Her eyes fluttered closed, heavy with exhaustion. As the world faded away, Grace told herself not to overthink things, to just let herself feel good for once.

Something was tugging on her hair.

Grace blinked her eyes open.

Hunter gave her a guilty look. "Please don't tell me I woke you up."

"What's wrong?"

"Nothing is wrong. It's perfect, in fact. It's just that my arm has gone numb." He grunted and shifted slightly.

"Oh!" Grace lifted her head, and he pulled his arm out.

Hunter settled back down next to her, draping his other arm over her midsection. "Now it's really perfect."

She nuzzled him, breathing in his familiar musky scent. "What did we just do?"

"What we should've been doing this whole time."

Grace poked his abs. "You're silly."

"The only silly thing was not making you feel like the most important person on Earth every single day I woke up with you."

She lifted herself up on her elbow to look at him. "Don't do that, Hunter. Not now."

"Don't do what?"

Her throat grew tight. Why couldn't they just be normal? It wasn't fair to love someone so much, knowing how much he could hurt her. "Don't make me fall back in love with you."

"What about you? Can you do me a favor and stop being irresistible?"

She lay back down, pulling the blanket up to her chin. As

if she could stop any of this. Look at what had happened to her good intentions.

He played with her hair. "What are you thinking about?"

"What makes you think I'm thinking about anything?"

"Because you're always thinking. "

She smiled into his chest. "We're quite a pair, huh? Me overthinking, you never thinking at all."

"Hey, give me some credit. I think about things in the moment."

She bit her lip. Hunter had told her that the way to get the truth out of a guy was to ask him after sleeping together. Here was her chance to test that theory. "So I take it you haven't thought about what happens now? After this?"

"Actually, I have. I was hoping it would happen again."

Grace swallowed. "You know what I mean."

"Will you settle for me telling you how I feel?"

She rolled over, propping herself up on her elbows and resting her chin on her clasped hands. "You're kidding, right? A woman never passes on the chance to hear a man's feelings. My love life might have been nonexistent for the past two years, but I've read enough romance books in my lifetime to know that for sure."

"Oh God, no pressure." He tucked a strand of hair behind her ear. "I still care about you, Grace. A lot. You're the only one for me."

Her heart sank. "But."

"There is no but."

"Oh, really? Then tell me how this is going to work. With me here and you, well, everywhere else."

Hunter looked her in the eye. "I screwed this up once before. I won't do it again. I'll stay. I'll figure something out."

Her heart pounded in her ears as she asked her next question, already afraid of the answer. "Are you sure you don't want me to go with you again? How it used to be? Isn't that better than you staying here? It will cost you more to stay than it would for me to leave."

He reached out to caress her cheek. "Nope. Last time, my career cost me you. Not worth it. Besides, when have I ever missed your birthday?"

She lifted the corner of her mouth. "The last two years."

"Can we chalk that up to me being an idiot?" Hunter sighed. "And it's not every day that my wife turns forty. I've been looking forward to those senior citizen discounts for a while."

Grace flopped down beside him again. "It's really not fair that you're six months younger than me, you know that?"

He pulled her close. "I'll follow you into the next decade soon enough. For now, can't you enjoy being with a younger man?"

"That I can do." Her heart stretched in her chest. Being with Hunter felt so natural. So right. It was like something had been missing this whole time, only she wasn't sure what it was until she got it back.

Grace had thought pigs would fly before Hunter ever gave up his lifestyle. Even now, she had no idea how he would pull it off. But her heart begged her to believe him. Just this once.

After all, he hadn't lied to her yet.

CHAPTER SIXTEEN

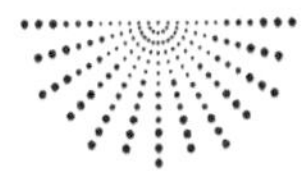

GRACE

"Now can we get to the fun stuff? Please?" Vivian wheezed.

Grace grunted as they set down the hundred-pound bag of coffee beans. Delivery day inevitably doubled as workout day. "Work before play."

Vivian glanced at the clipboard. "Then it's time for play because that's the last of it. Although I still think you should've asked Hunter to do the heavy lifting."

Grace ran the back of her hand across her forehead, wiping away the sweat. She had the same thought. But she was toeing a dangerous line, and the more she came to depend on Hunter being there, the thinner the line got. "We never needed him before."

"Speak for yourself." Vivian waved a slender arm. "Do I look like someone who picks up heavy things for fun?"

"No need to flaunt your great figure in my face, okay?" Grace teased. "How the heck you bake like a French pastry chef and still look like that is beyond me. I'd eat everything I made."

Vivian rolled her eyes. "Says the lady with the sexy husband."

"Let me stop you right there." Grace held up a hand. "We aren't anything. You know what? I'd rather talk about the party."

Vivian grinned. "Fantastic."

"You are being a very bad introvert right now," Grace muttered as they walked from the storage room to the front of the coffee shop.

"It's your fortieth birthday. You're my friend. Of course I'm excited. I'm excited that you're turning forty way before me."

Grace let out a laugh and moved the bell from the counter. Then, she poured two glasses of iced tea, adding a lemon wedge to the rim of each one. "I bet no one knows what a great sense of humor you have." She carried the glasses over to the bistro table where Vivian waited. Grace set them down, counting off on her fingers. "Plus, you're funny, kind, smart. How are you still single?"

Vivian held up her own fingers. "One, Alaska. Two, I want to be."

Grace countered with a single finger. "One day, that might change."

Vivian reached for her tea, her face as sour as if she had taken a chomp out of the lemon wedge. "Trust me, it won't."

As with Hunter, Grace sensed that the discussion was closed. She could respect that. She and Vivian had an unspoken understanding that some subjects were off-limits. "Okay, I think the party is the only safe topic we have left."

Vivian gave her a smug look. "Victory is mine."

Grace spread her hands on the table. "Look, I just don't want you to be disappointed when no one shows up."

"Are you kidding?" Vivian gaped at her. "Something to do

in Darling? Not to mention that everyone likes you. It'll be a full house."

Grace took a sip of her tea. She enjoyed chatting with everyone who came through the doors of the Driftwood, but she wasn't delusional. People came to the coffee shop because it was one of two options in town. Then again, her birthday party would probably be one of one option for something to do that night. Maybe Vivian was right. "Should we have it at the Buck, in that case? We should probably clear it with Wolfie beforehand."

She still felt a tiny bit guilty that she had passed Hunter off onto the Buck when he first got there. Not that anyone else seemed to think twice about it. Hunter and Wolfie acted like old friends already.

Besides, Hunter had spent more and more time at the coffee shop the past few days. Grace had thought it might be weird to be around each other so much again. But the only weird thing was how natural it felt.

Vivian scrolled through the calendar app on her phone. "Yeah. That gives Wolfie two weeks to order what he needs."

"Okay. I'll go over there after we decide on everything else. Do you think people will mind if the food is vegetarian?"

"Not as long as there is beer. The good news is that Wolfie doesn't have to order extra of that."

Next, they estimated how many people would be there, how much food they'd need, and how many drinks per person to plan for. Vivian had a few boxes of decorations they could use, and she was pretty sure the Buck had some too. As far as music, the jukebox would have to do. Wolfie kept a jar of quarters by the machine so people could make their own playlist as the night went on.

If only Grace could think about the jukebox without

thinking about Hunter. Which led to thinking about Hunter without a shirt on.

The room suddenly seemed too warm, and she took a gulp of her iced tea. Hopefully, her face wasn't red.

Vivian passed the list across the table. "I think that's everything."

Grace read it over a second time. If they had this party anywhere else, it would involve professional catering, a bartender for hire, a DJ, and more. All for a ridiculous amount of money. She liked this version so much better, even if no one came. "Looks perfect to me."

"What are you wearing?"

Grace glanced down at her jeans and T-shirt. "What I always wear. Probably some variation of this."

"No way. You aren't getting off that easy. This is your party. Don't you want to look amazing?"

Grace plucked at her shirt. "This is how everyone here dresses. If I don't wear flannel, I'll stand out from the crowd."

"We can order something." Vivian picked up her phone.

"Nothing I order online ever fits. I'm a giant."

Vivian snorted. "I hope you don't expect me to feel bad for you because you have the height and looks of a model. But if you don't want to order online, why not go to Juneau to get something new?"

Grace shook her head. "You know this place is open six days a week. A turnaround trip to Juneau doesn't leave much time to shop. It's pointless."

"So close it, or Hunter can serve drip coffee and hot tea for the day. No one in town will bat an eye."

Grace gave her a look. "You know, when I first met you, I thought you were this quiet, sweet little thing. Now I find out you are a total firecracker."

"Only for people I care about." Vivian grinned. "Are we going or not?"

Grace sighed. "I will go if you come with me. You're the whole reason I'm even considering this crazy idea. But I need to talk to Hunter about watching the coffee shop first."

Vivian glanced around. "Where is the famous Mr. Hart, anyway?"

"On a run." Preserving his stupid, perfect body. The man hadn't aged a day. If Hunter was ever in the mood for a career change, he was a shoo-in as a romance book cover model. It really wasn't fair.

Her stomach twisted. It also wasn't fair that less than two weeks together made her forget all the reasons why she hated him. Especially when they were exactly three weeks away from being officially divorced. Grace could have all the time in the world and still not untangle her feelings about Hunter. How the heck was she supposed to figure it out in less than a month?

Grace stood, needing to keep her body, and mind, busy. "I better get going on that inventory."

"Let me know what you want to do about Juneau." Vivian got up too, pausing briefly to scratch Ruby's ears. "I'm heading out."

After Vivian left, Grace set the bell on the counter again and went to the back of the shop to work on the inventory. It was an unusually quiet day, and Grace intended to take full advantage of it to finish the task at hand.

If only her mind would cooperate. The numbers and letters on the clipboard swirled around, and all she could think about was Hunter's ridiculous abs.

Screw him.

Screw him for coming here and reminding her of how good life could be.

Screw him for being handsome and kind and fun.

Screw him for being impossible not to love.

Her shoulders sagged.

Screw her for depending on him.

Screw her for trusting him.

Grace had felt him looking at her. She had heard the questions he hadn't asked. Ever since that night together, he was waiting for her to give him a sign. Did she want this too? Or was it a mistake?

Of course she wanted it. Wanted them. There had been no one else her entire life. Only Hunter.

She didn't doubt that he loved her too. They'd always been loyal to each other since the beginning. Grace was certain of it, even with the hours Hunter spent photographing the most beautiful women in the world.

But he also loved his career. In Hunter's line of work, the kind of life Grace wanted wasn't just hard. It was impossible. There was no such thing as normal. A permanent address only held a person back. A family was a liability. The only consistency was change.

If Grace had learned nothing else during their marriage, it was that Hunter's career always came first. Back then, she hadn't minded being in the background of his work. She didn't need the spotlight on her. She didn't even like it. Until she realized that she had faded away altogether.

It wasn't just Grace who faded into the background. It was her dreams. Her wants. Her needs. Hunter had always assured her they would have time to do it all.

Then one day, time ran out.

After they separated, it didn't take long for any doubts Grace had to evaporate. When she had looked him up online, any news was only about Hunter and his work. Just like it always had been. His broken marriage didn't even merit a mention.

Hunter had told her he wanted her back. That things would be different this time. Grace's heart ached, wishing she could believe him. But years of doubt didn't disappear overnight. Especially not when she knew better. If Grace got lost in him again, there would be no one to blame but herself.

The bell over the door chimed faintly, and she snapped her head up. Great. She had been so busy wallowing in self-pity that she had missed her chance to work on the inventory when the shop was quiet.

"Grace?"

She cleared her throat. Speak of the devil. Or angel, depending on the day and the presence of the dimple. "Back here!"

Hunter popped his head into the storage room, Ruby following him, of course. The dog didn't share Grace's reservations about Hunter. "What are you up to?"

She gestured to the bags of coffee beans. "Inventory."

He frowned. "Why didn't you let me know? I could've helped."

"Just used to doing things without you, I guess."

He stepped into the room, and her body heated up. He should look disgusting, dripping with sweat. But it took everything Grace had not to drag him upstairs. What did they say? Absence made the heart grow fonder? Yeah, well, it had definitely turbocharged her body's reaction to his. "Well, get used to me being around. The next time you need help, promise you'll ask."

She tapped the pen against the clipboard. As long as he was offering. "Actually, there is something."

"Anything."

"Vivian suggested a trip to Juneau to get a new outfit for my birthday. But I would either have to close the Driftwood, or you could run it for the day. Only if you don't mind, of course."

"Would you feel better if we kept it open?"

Grace shifted her feet. Why not tell him what she

honestly wanted? Maybe their marriage wouldn't have fallen apart if she had done that more often. "Kinda."

He smiled. "Then we'll keep it open. Just show me how to make the coffee and all that, and I'll take care of it."

"You really don't mind? You don't have to do it."

"Anything for my wife." Hunter kissed her forehead. "I'll try not to burn the coffee."

She leaned back, peering at him. "You remember the part where we signed divorce papers, right?"

"How could I forget?" He placed his hand over his heart in mock pain. "My job is to make you remember why you married me in the first place."

Grace bit her lip. Damn him. It was impossible to stay mad at him. She turned back towards the shelves, hoping that she could focus better without Hunter in sight. It was futile. "How was your jog?"

"Good. Except I feel sweaty and gross. I'm going to jump in the shower, and then I can help with whatever you need."

No, he wasn't. It would be easier if he were gross. "It's all yours."

"Any chance you could join me?"

Her stomach fluttered. *Can't* and *want* were two different things. "Nope. I need to finish the inventory before it gets busy, and I have to work late."

Hunter came up behind her, wrapping his arms around her waist. "Then how about I make you a deal? I'll go shower, alone. Then I'll come down here and help you. And then I'll make dinner. That way, no one has to work late."

She closed her eyes. How dare he be so wonderful. How dare she fall for him again.

Grace's stomach let out a growl, and she snapped her eyes open. It seemed that her heart and her stomach were in cahoots. Hopefully, her brain didn't join ranks with them, or she'd really be out of luck.

Hunter gave her a squeeze. "Make that a very early dinner."

"Don't worry about it. I'm fine."

"Hey," he said softly. "Is something wrong?"

Grace swallowed. Nothing was wrong. Everything was right. And that was the problem. "What about when you leave again? We both know you will."

Hunter placed his hands on her shoulders and gently turned her to face him. "Is that what is bothering you? Grace, I told you. I want to make this work. I'm in it to win it."

"And the divorce papers? You know, the ones that will be finalized in mere weeks?"

"We'll tear them up. Or however you un-divorce someone."

She let out a huff. "Do you have to be so lovable? It makes it really hard to stay mad at you."

"Would you prefer that I'm not? Maybe I should let my dirty laundry pile up? Give you the silent treatment? Something like that?"

Grace bit the inside of her cheek to keep from smiling. No. She wouldn't give in that easy. He would have to earn her smiles. "Screw you."

His eyes turned to the color of a stormy sky. "Now you're talking."

"Seriously, Hunter. Who else can go from mitigating a breakdown to flirting in thirty seconds flat?"

"That's what I keep telling you. You'd be bored with anyone else." He winked. "Now, what are you in the mood for? Grilled cheese? A cold cheese sandwich? That's pretty much the limit of my cooking skills, unless you count eating the bread and cheese separately."

She giggled. "I seem to remember some really delicious chips and dip we had once."

"Store-bought. All of it."

"Grilled cheese it is, then."

"I'll be right back." He paused in the doorway, looking her in the eye. "And for the record? I'm not going anywhere. Trust me, Grace. I won't screw it up this time."

Ruby followed him, her nails clicking on the wooden stairs paired with Hunter's heavy footsteps.

Grace tried to focus on the inventory one more time, but she had lost her spot again. Maybe she should just do it tomorrow.

Love and fear swirled in her stomach. She rested a hand on her tummy. Maybe she was just hungry. Didn't people get emotional when they were hungry?

That must be it. Because Hunter was wonderful, right? After all, she fell in love with him once before. She must've had her reasons. Not just his damn dimple and gray eyes. And now he was telling her everything she ever wanted to hear.

But Grace couldn't ignore the unease that snaked through her heart, leaving a cold trail that led to all of her worst memories and biggest fears.

That she loved Hunter too much. That she loved him more than he could ever love her. And that he could never give her what she wanted, no matter what promises he made.

Her throat tightened. No, the problem wasn't falling in love with him again. It was falling out of love.

Walking away from Hunter had been the hardest thing she ever did. Grace wasn't sure she could do it again.

CHAPTER SEVENTEEN

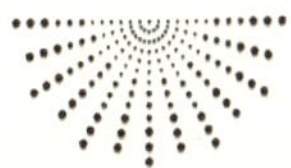

GRACE

If there was one thing that Grace could appreciate about her old life with Hunter, it was that she almost never had to dress up. Of course, there was more that she had enjoyed about that time, despite her frustrations. Grace wouldn't have stuck around so long if it had been all bad. But not dressing up was what came to mind as she flicked through the clothing racks at the mall.

Grace sighed. "I already wasn't excited about the idea of coming to Juneau, but it's even less exciting to come all this way for nothing."

Vivian plucked a dress from the rack, holding it up to Grace before shaking her head and hanging it up again. "I refuse to go back empty-handed."

"I'd be happy just to go back," Grace mumbled. She pulled her phone from her purse. No missed calls from Hunter. Was that a good sign? No calls probably meant no problems. After all, Hunter had been in Darling for two weeks. He wasn't completely unfamiliar with the routine at the coffee shop.

She wrinkled her forehead. Or it meant a problem so huge that he didn't have time to tell her about it. Or didn't want to. "Maybe I should call Hunter. Just to check in."

Vivian gave her a look. "It's fine, Grace. You know how Darling is. If Hunter burns the coffee, someone will just climb behind the counter and fix it for him."

Grace put her phone away. "I know that's supposed to help me feel better, but it just makes me question why people buy coffee from me at all." She shook her head. "Sometimes I wonder why I thought the Driftwood was a good idea. It never occurred to me that the reason there wasn't already a coffee shop in the middle of nowhere was perhaps because you didn't need one."

"Of course we need a coffee shop. We'll take whatever we can get."

"Heartwarming," Grace said dryly. "And you don't even drink coffee. Not really a reliable source."

"What I wonder is why you think this is only about the coffee? We all love having you in Darling. My social life has definitely improved."

"I like hanging out with you too." She shot Vivian a teasing smile. "Most of the time. Just not when you drag me to Juneau."

"Ha-ha. How about a little less joking and a little more dress shopping?"

With a mock pout, Grace turned back to the rack to continue her search. Yes, she definitely counted Vivian as a friend. But as far as why the coffee shop was popular? That seemed obvious to Grace. People came to the Driftwood because it was something to do in a town that didn't offer much else.

But what if Vivian was right? What if it was more about Grace than the coffee? What if everyone liked her as much as she liked them?

Grace had opened the Driftwood because she hadn't had any other work experience besides making coffee. But it had become so much more than that.

What if you already have everything you ever wanted?

Goose bumps rose along her arms at the memory of Natasha's words. Was it possible the older woman had been right?

Grace regretted not finishing her business degree, but she still had a business, didn't she? She had wanted a home. Friends. A normal life that was stable and predictable and familiar. She had all that and more.

Though maybe normal wasn't the right word to describe life in Darling. The only restaurant in town didn't charge people, Grace had to take a boat to go dress shopping, and no one locked their cars.

None of that changed the truth. The Driftwood, and Darling, had started off as her only option. Now, there was nowhere else she'd rather be.

Her heart skipped a beat. And no one else she'd rather be with than Hunter.

Hunter, who wanted her back. Hunter, who had always been the only one for her, even if she didn't always think she was the right one for him. Hunter, who had stepped up for her so that she wouldn't worry about the coffee shop when she was in Juneau.

Grace loved her independence. She had earned it. But the truth was that life was so much better with Hunter in it.

Maybe she hadn't been lost in Hunter. Maybe she had been found.

"You know, I think you're onto something with the coffee shop," Vivian mused, interrupting her thoughts.

Grace blinked. "What do you mean? You think I should check in on Hunter?"

"Not that. What you said about having a place in the

middle of nowhere. It was something completely different from what you had been doing before, right?"

"That's putting it mildly."

"Then I know what we need to do." Vivian abandoned the rack she had been looking at. "Follow me."

Grace trailed behind her as they walked through the store. They flew by more than one dress that seemed like a good candidate. Long, flowy things that were more comfortable than fashionable. "Slow down. There are a few back there that I want to look at."

"They aren't right. Trust me."

"And how do you know that?"

Vivian stopped so suddenly that Grace almost crashed into her. "That's it."

Grace followed her friend's gaze, and her eyes widened. No. No way. Vivian couldn't possibly be talking about *that* dress? It wasn't even a dress. It was just a skimpy piece of fabric that probably needed to be held on with double-sided tape, a trick Grace had learned from Hunter's photoshoots. "Are you joking?"

Vivian reached for the dress, pressing it into Grace's hands and ushering her into a fitting room. "Not at all. Just try it on."

Grace planted her feet. "I will try it on under one condition. After this, I am done shopping, with or without an outfit."

Vivian didn't hesitate. "Deal."

Grace peered at her. "Your confidence is a bit unnerving. But the idea of being done with shopping is too tempting to pass up."

With renewed hope, Grace closed the door of the fitting room behind her. She hung her purse up on a hook before shedding her jeans and sweatshirt, shimmying into the dress.

She shook her head as she tugged on the skimpy scrap of

fabric. Thank goodness Vivian was the only one here to witness this fashion crime. The dress looked like it was meant for a nightclub, not a bar in Alaska. And definitely not a forty-year-old's birthday.

Grace straightened, smoothing out the dress and looking in the mirror.

Her jaw dropped. God damn. Vivian had been right.

The fabric fell perfectly over Grace's figure, making her look both slender and toned. The shimmer cast a warm glow that was flattering even in the garish fluorescent dressing room light. And the pink color was reminiscent of the *Open* sign at the coffee shop.

She turned from side to side in front of the mirror.

Holy cow. She looked amazing.

A knock came at the fitting room door. "Everything okay in there?"

With a deep breath, Grace opened the door. "What do you think?"

Vivian gave her a smug smile. "I think you must be glad you tried it on. You're a total knockout."

Grace bit her lip. "Don't you think it's a little too much for the Buck?"

"Too much to celebrate your own birthday? Impossible."

Grace looked in the mirror again. She did love it. "How did you know it would work?"

"It was your idea, actually. You said the coffee shop was something completely different. Why not do the same thing for the dress? Sometimes you have to try something you would never normally do in order to find something that works."

Grace's heart seemed to stop as she stared at her reflection.

Something she would never normally do.

Something like give Hunter a second chance. Something like believe him.

After all, didn't he do something out of the blue too? He came here to grieve and to heal from his loss. But his presence in Darling had healed things between them too.

Grace had been so bitter, so resentful, at the end of their relationship that all those angry feelings had buried every good memory. But there *were* good memories. In fact, they were mostly good. And was it really fair to blame Hunter for something he didn't know?

She turned to look at Vivian. "I think I've decided."

Vivian's face lit up. "About the dress?"

Grace smiled. No wonder the dating app had been a bust. Her Prince Charming had been there the entire time. "About everything."

CHAPTER EIGHTEEN

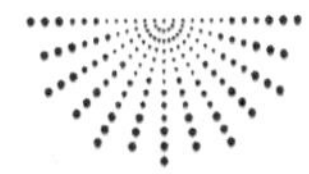

HUNTER

It was a good thing that Hunter Hart was a photographer. Because he definitely didn't have a future as a barista.

He held a mug under the airpot and pressed down, only for the contraption to let out a pathetic wheeze. Not even so much as a single drop of coffee came out.

Hunter cursed under his breath. He was supposed to make more coffee after the last customer. But he only remembered when he came back to the empty airpot. After two weeks of living at a coffee shop, he thought he would've done better at running things.

He glanced at the fisherman who stood on the other side of the counter. "Sorry. I need to make more."

The guy lifted a shoulder. "I can wait."

"Thanks. It'll only be a few minutes." Hunter opened up the cabinets, searching for the coffee grounds. He had just made coffee this morning. He should be able to find it quickly.

Unfortunately, Hunter seemed to have developed

amnesia between this morning and now. Perhaps a side effect of getting up so early and going nonstop ever since. How the heck did Grace do it?

He muttered another curse as he looked in the next cabinet. Still no coffee.

The fisherman coughed. "Out for the day, huh?"

Hunter glanced at the espresso machine. That was always an option. But after Grace attempted to show him how to pull a shot five separate times, they had decided that he was better off sticking with drip coffee and hot tea for the day.

He turned back to the fisherman. "I think I am. But Grace will be back tomorrow."

"Then so will I." The guy flashed him a crooked smile. "In the meantime, I'm going to head to the Buck. Want anything?"

Hunter couldn't help but smile back. This had to be the only place on Earth where a person could completely botch the job, and no one cared. Not only did they not care, they were nice about it. Definitely not what Hunter had expected when the grizzled fisherman first walked in. "No, thanks, but I appreciate it. I'm going to be back here, cleaning up and looking for my pride."

The man chuckled and headed across the street.

Hunter rang up a coffee and ran his own credit card through the machine. He wasn't much help when it came to making drinks, but he could at least make sure Grace turned a profit for the day.

He tucked his credit card back into his wallet. Why didn't he think of doing that in the first place? Then Grace would've still had a good day of business, and he wouldn't have possibly tanked the reputation of the Driftwood.

Rubbing the back of his neck, Hunter took in the mess. How had he screwed things up so badly in just a day? And how the heck was he going to put the Driftwood back together? But he had to. Grace would be returning this evening.

Hopefully. If not, Darling would be going through a collective caffeine withdrawal.

Hunter looked at Ruby, who was perched prettily on her dog bed. "You better not tell her how bad it was."

Ruby blinked at him.

Hunter sighed. "You're right. She's going to know."

He grabbed a cleaning rag and started with the back counter. It was definitely in the worst condition, covered in coffee grounds, splashes of milk, and dirty dishes. If he got that done, maybe the rest of the place wouldn't seem so bad.

The bell chimed over the door, and Hunter's shoulders pinched together.

It better not be Wolfie again. The barkeep had already come across the street to check on Hunter so many times that he was beginning to think the Buck must be closed for business today.

Still, Hunter wasn't about to snap the older man's head off. They might not be as close as he and Jack had been, but after Hunter had worked at the Buck his first week or so in Darling, Wolfie had become more of a friend than anyone Hunter had met in the last decade. And he wasn't in a position to be losing the few friends he had.

Hunter pasted on a smile before turning around. But his face fell when he saw who stood on the other side of the counter. "Oh no. I can't in good faith serve you coffee. It would be an insult to your taste buds."

Elle laughed. "Actually, I just came by to grab a refill for my machine at home. Whole bean, please, not ground."

Hunter let out a deep breath. That was the best news he had heard all day. "You want to buy coffee I didn't make? You're my new favorite customer."

"Don't tell Mac. I'm pretty sure he thinks he is the

favorite customer. He takes pride in being the first one in here every morning."

Hunter rang up the bag of coffee. The bearded giant had indeed been the first one in this morning. "So in that case, why are you buying these? Can't he pick you up something to drink when he comes in?"

She handed Hunter her credit card. "Because unlike Mac, I like to sleep until a normal human time. Not to mention, one cup wouldn't be enough. My entire business is pretty much powered by coffee. I sip on it all morning while I'm working."

Hunter nodded. That sounded familiar. When he was editing, the entire day could pass by without him getting off his computer. He wouldn't have anything to eat besides black coffee until he either finished working or someone finally forced him away from his computer. "I understand what it's like to get in the zone like that."

Elle tucked the bag of coffee beans under her arm. "Especially here. No distractions." Her face pinched together. "Not even when you want one."

He chuckled. "So that's the secret to productivity, huh? Live in Darling?"

"Maybe. Now that I've made the move, I can't imagine being anywhere else. I'm sure you can relate, but nothing used to be more important to me than work. Until I realized there is no one right way to be successful. Just one right person to be successful with." Elle grimaced. "I know it sounds cheesy. But it's true."

"It doesn't sound cheesy at all."

Especially since he had recently come to the same conclusion himself. Only unlike Elle, he had destroyed his marriage before he had figured it out. But Hunter didn't care how many days of hard work he had to do at the Driftwood. He was determined to make things right with Grace and rebuild their life together.

Except he didn't have an unlimited amount of time. There were two weeks left until the divorce was finalized. Which meant every day counted. Maybe Elle had some insights that could save him precious time. "Out of curiosity, which came first? Meeting Mac or moving to Darling?"

Her eyes danced with laughter. "Technically, meeting and hating Mac came first. Then I fell for him and for Darling. But I still went back to California. Mac had to come and get me. We've never been apart since."

Hunter whistled. "Sounds like the long way around." He knew something about that.

"It was worth it to get my happily ever after." Elle beamed. "Thanks again. I'll see you around."

After she left, Hunter checked the time. His knees almost buckled in relief. Oh, thank God. It was two minutes after two.

He lunged across the coffee shop and flicked off the *Open* sign with the kind of enthusiasm usually reserved for carrying the Olympic torch. Fittingly, Hunter felt like he had just run a marathon.

He cracked his neck, overwhelmed by everything he still had to do. He really had no idea how Grace did this every day.

Hunter had met a lot of incredible people, thanks to his career. Scientists. Athletes. Movie stars. None of them held a candle to Grace. He had known from the moment he met her that no one else would ever come close. And Hunter never intended to forget that again.

As he wiped down the counters, he could hear Jack saying that he'd finally gotten his head on straight and that it was about damn time too.

But then when Hunter tried to picture telling Dana that

he wanted to keep Darling as a home base, he heard her calling him an idiot.

He straightened. No one else's opinion mattered. What mattered was what he and Grace wanted.

Ruby walked up to him, letting out a whine.

With a sigh, Hunter tossed the cleaning rag in the sink. Right. It was time for her walk. His brain seemed to have filed that information in the same place as remembering to make more coffee and where Grace kept said coffee.

The bell chimed over the door, but this time, Hunter didn't panic. They were closed for the day. He couldn't mess up an order if he wasn't taking them anymore.

"Oh. My. God."

He whipped around, seeing spots. So much for not panicking. "Grace? You're back already?"

"We took an earlier ferry." She held a shopping bag in one hand, her duffel bag in the other. "By the looks of things, I'm not back early enough."

"You should've been here an hour ago. It was worse."

As soon as the words were out of his mouth, Hunter regretted them. That was probably the last thing Grace wanted to hear. But her face softened in apparent sympathy. "It sounds like a hard day. I know what that's like. I can't believe you kept it open."

"It's what you wanted. I know how important this place is to you."

Grace took a step closer. "Actually, you're wrong."

He wrinkled his forehead. "I am?"

"Well, and you're right. This place is important to me. But not more important than you." Her mouth curved into a smile. "In fact, I am struggling to remember what is."

Hunter's head spun. Was he dreaming? Delirious from his crazy day, maybe? Because her words were music to his ears. If he was dreaming, he didn't want to wake up. "I should've offered to take over the coffee shop on my first day here. Then I wouldn't have a panic attack every time I looked at the calendar and realized we were one day closer to the divorce."

"Saying something and doing something are very different."

"I'd do anything for you."

She held his gaze. "I know."

Hunter walked out from behind the counter and wrapped her in a hug, squishing the bags to her side. "I don't know what the heck happened in Juneau, but I couldn't be happier. Except if you tell me I never have to do this again."

Grace shook with a laugh. "Deal. Next time, you can come with me. It's better with you." Her voice grew quiet. "Everything is better with you."

His heart stretched in his chest. His thoughts exactly.

CHAPTER NINETEEN

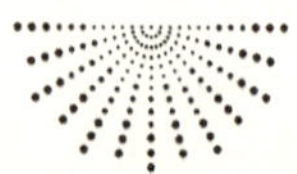

GRACE

Finally, she had a chance.

Grace rinsed out the frothing tin and set it aside. The coffee shop had been nonstop all day. In fact, the entire last week had been busier than usual.

Hunter had apologized more than once for failing miserably at running the Driftwood. His words. But in one of life's ironic twists, it turned out that a reminder of Darling without decent coffee had reinvigorated business.

Grace smiled to herself as she wiped her hands on her apron and gave Ruby a quick pat on her head. The town wasn't the only one who was reinvigorated by Hunter's presence. Grace had a new appreciation for everything, and everyone, in her life.

And after thinking about it for the past week, it was time to call the attorney.

Grace flicked off the *Open* sign and pulled her cell phone from her back pocket. She had no idea what was involved in canceling a divorce, but that's what attorneys were for. All she knew was that separating from Hunter wasn't what she wanted. Not right now. Maybe not ever.

Before the phone even started ringing, she was interrupted again.

"Grace?" Hunter called out, followed by the stairs creaking under his weight. "Do you have a minute?"

With a sigh, Grace shoved her phone back into her pocket. She'd ask Hunter if he could wait until she made her phone call. He'd understand when she told him what it was about.

But the phone call was forgotten the minute she saw the look on his face.

She told herself there was no reason to be nervous. There was no reason for her stomach to sink, for her heart to pound in her ears. But just because there was no reason didn't change how she felt. "What is it?"

"Dana called."

Dread crept through her. So it was about his work. His work far away from Darling. "Where do you have to go?"

"Just promise you'll give me a chance to explain." He ran a hand through his hair. "There's a job in Sedona."

Her breath caught for a moment. Jack's hometown. "When?"

Hunter shifted to his other foot. "In a week."

"Oh."

"I think I could still be back in time for your birthday. *If* I take it."

Grace swallowed, trying to hold herself together. There had been other job offers that Hunter hadn't even been tempted by. But this one was different.

She could understand why. Because of Jack. And if Hunter left for a few days, it didn't mean he wasn't coming back. "Of course you have to take it."

He knit his brows together. "Do I? Jack is gone. It still

breaks my heart every time I think about it. But if he were alive, I know he'd say that I should stay here with you." Hunter's mouth quirked up. "He never missed the chance to tell me how stupid I was to let you go."

"I always liked Jack." She meant it to be lighthearted, but her voice cracked. Grace looked away, blinking furiously.

"Grace? What's wrong?"

"It's just, what if—" Sobs choked off the rest of her words.

In an instant, Hunter was next to her, wrapping her in his stupid, muscled arms as she leaned against his stupid, muscled chest. He held her while she cried, soaking his shirt with tears.

Grace cried for the young, naive woman who believed in the man holding her. She cried for not trusting herself. She cried until she had nothing left.

The idea of Hunter leaving, even for a few days, shoved its fingers in a wound that had never fully healed. How long had she craved a home? A family? For a while, she had thought she had that with Hunter. They were young and in love. The home would come with time. The family would come with time. But in the end, they never had.

"How does it still hurt?" Her voice was raw.

Hunter smoothed her hair, his touch soothing. "Grace, I swear to you, as long as I'm alive, I'll try to make it better. It's not too late."

"Not for you." She wiped at her nose. "Biology is so much kinder to men."

"Yeah. Being a woman seems like it sucks."

She snorted. "Thanks for agreeing with me. If you can't make things right, at least tell me I'm right."

"I'll get that cross-stitched on a pillow so I never forget."

She choked on a laugh. "I hate you."

"I'm getting mixed signals here, honey."

She stepped back to look up at him. "You're impossible to stay mad at. Do you know that?"

He grinned. "It's my secret weapon."

Ruby whined, pacing by the door.

"I'm going to take her out," Hunter said. "Don't go anywhere."

Grace eyed the full dish bins, her body sagging with exhaustion. "Unlikely."

"I'll help you when I get back. And then I'm making you dinner. Hope you like peanut butter from the jar." He brushed a kiss to her cheek before disappearing outside with Ruby.

Grace sucked in a deep breath. She needed a minute to herself. It was good Hunter had taken Ruby out.

Her feet ached. Her hands were chapped from washing dishes. And she hadn't sat down once. When Grace checked the tally for the end of the day, her eyes nearly watered. It was what she usually made in a week. No wonder she was tuckered out.

Normally, cleaning up was the perfect distraction. If only her brain wasn't a dog with a bone.

Hunter was leaving. She was sure of it. He said he would come back. But what if he didn't?

She had just finished wiping down the counter when Hunter returned, his face sweaty.

Sweaty and delicious.

Stupid brain.

Grace cleared her throat. "Did you do laps around the island or something?"

Hunter pointed at Ruby. "I decided to squeeze in some cardio and try to keep up with this one while she ran after the waves. Turns out the dog is in better shape than I am."

Grace wrung the rag out over the sink, her arms weak after the long day. She had a million reasons to not love

Hunter. If only not loving him was an option. "Thanks for taking her out. I was slammed today."

"Happy to." He came up behind Grace and pressed a kiss to the crown of her head. "Now, how about that dinner I promised you?"

"It's fine, really. I can make something." She turned and found herself nose-to-nose with Hunter. He was so close that she could see the faint freckles on his forehead.

His eyes crinkled at the corners. "Ah, Grace. When are you going to learn to believe my promises?"

Her heart hid behind her mind. Believing him wasn't the hard part. It was being disappointed.

CHAPTER TWENTY

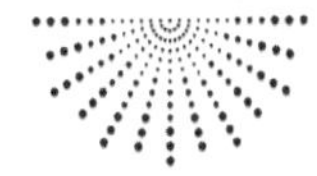

HUNTER

Hunter checked his phone to see another missed call. The fifth one today.

His head throbbed. He still hadn't given Dana an answer on the Sedona job. It wasn't right. Dana had been covering him for a month now. The least he could do was to make a decision.

Not that she would ever complain. Dana was tireless, but more than that, she really did care about Hunter. The feeling was mutual and probably the reason their business partnership had lasted so long. He couldn't imagine working with someone who treated him as nothing more than a tireless cash cow. He was lucky to have Dana, and just as with Grace, he should treat her like it.

Guilt curled in his stomach. He hadn't told Dana about staying in Darling. He had never kept something like that from her before.

Oh, Hunter was spontaneous. He didn't usually think through his decisions before making them, let alone talk them out. But he at least updated Dana as he went along, keeping her more or less in the loop. They were a team, after all.

It was about more than work. Dana was also protective of Hunter. She had seen him limp through heartbreak after things ended with Grace the first time. Would Dana understand that Hunter couldn't, wouldn't walk away from Grace? Not now. Not after being with her again.

Aunt Linda had always told Hunter that actions spoke louder than words. It was time to show Grace how much he cared, and that meant putting some skin in the game.

His phone vibrated again, inching across the bistro table. The Driftwood had become his regular workspace, though he still made regular stops by the Buck to chat with Wolfie. Hunter also often took Ruby for a midday walk when Grace was working. While he could happily spend every minute of every day around Grace, he was trying not to push the envelope. Hunter had a feeling she could easily toss him out on his ass again if he didn't respect her boundaries.

"If you don't answer it this time, I will. It's starting to sound like the coffee shop has a buzzing phone soundtrack," Grace snapped, slamming a cabinet door shut.

Hunter darted his arm out, grabbing the phone. Grace had been exhausted every night after work for the past week, and as a result, she didn't have much patience. His best form of defense had been to evade conflict whenever possible.

His back ached as he looked at the caller ID. Besides, it was time to face real life. It was now or never. And he didn't have that much time. "I'll be right back."

Slipping on his jacket, he stepped outside to answer the call.

"Hunter! God, it was easier to talk to you when you did Everest."

"Don't be dramatic, Dana." Hunter walked down Main

Street, his feet crunching on the gravel. "You know I'm not here for work. When's the last time I even took a vacation?"

She blew air into the phone. "Your life is a vacation. And does that mean I'm not allowed to worry about you or something? I know you've always done things your way, but you would at least check in once in a while. Between you being there and Lauren taking maternity leave, I feel like the last woman standing."

Hunter cringed. Oh, yeah. He had been so caught up in his own problems that he had forgotten his social media manager was going on maternity leave. He really did suck for not checking in with Dana more often. She always made sure he was okay. But did he ever ask her the same question? "I'll start posting my own stuff more often. And I'll call you." He perked up as he got another idea. "When's the last time you went on a date?"

Dana snorted. "Typical. You fall in love, and you start prescribing it to everyone else."

Hunter barked a laugh. "That's assuming there is a guy out there who can keep up with you."

"More like put up with me. And don't make promises you can't keep. I think the last time you posted to your own accounts is, oh, I don't know, never?"

His shoulders slumped forward as he reached the end of the street and turned in the direction of the waterfront. She was right. He didn't even know the passwords. Dana had set all that up years ago, insisting he needed a presence. "So what do you need me to do? I can send you some photos of Alaska to post if that helps."

"Really, it's fine. With you not having a lot of content right now, it makes it easier for me to do Lauren's job. Which is good because I have been very busy doing *my* job."

Hunter swallowed. It wasn't right to disappear on someone who had always stuck with him, no matter what bullshit he had pulled. Not to mention that he had been doing what he had been doing for so long, Hunter sometimes forgot it wasn't a guarantee his success would last forever. He was lucky and talented, sure, but he had to put in some effort on a regular basis too. "I'm sorry."

Dana was quiet for a moment. "Do you even want to do this anymore? You can tell me, kid. If you want a way out, we can find it."

He chewed on the inside of his cheek as he walked down to the water, the waves breaking against the beach with a crash. He couldn't imagine life without photography. But he couldn't imagine life without Grace either. Did the two have to be mutually exclusive? "I don't want to quit. I just— I don't know, maybe I need a slightly different fit."

"Good. Because that's why I called. I have news." She named one of the most renowned lifestyle magazines in the world and a salary that was nothing to shake a stick at. "Creative director."

Hunter's head spun. It was a job people worked towards their whole lives. It came with the kind of artistic control that made his mouth water. Not to mention a more stable schedule, something Grace would like. But it was in New York, far from Darling and his wife. "Are you serious?"

"Would I joke about this? It's my biggest win yet. They asked if you could give them an answer by the end of the month."

He stopped in his tracks, sending a few rocks skittering. The end of the month. Not exactly a lot of time to decide. But that shouldn't be a problem, right? They weren't going through with the divorce, or at least he was pretty sure they weren't. He needed to talk to Grace about that. And what better birthday present for her than a job that meant he could hopefully have more regular visits to Darling? But it wasn't a decision that Hunter could make on his own. "I need to talk to Grace."

Dana sighed, and Hunter braced himself. She always had his best interest at heart, even if it meant being a hard-ass at times. "I understand. But I don't think you're going to get a better offer than this. If you want to do something different, if you don't like this business anymore, we'll figure something else out. But if you do, this is as good as it gets. Trust me. I've been looking."

Hunter's heart was heavy as they ended the call. It was an incredible opportunity. Shouldn't he be jumping up and down right now?

He lowered himself onto the rocky beach, dragging his hand through the pebbles. Hunter felt like a baby. What was he so scared of? Dana was right. It was the offer of a lifetime. He wouldn't get a second chance at a job like this.

He was still grieving Jack, but it was more than that. Hunter was also grieving the life he used to live. He hadn't planned to make a career change when he came to Darling. He wasn't sure what the hell he was going to do. But with that offer Dana had brought up, Hunter realized that maybe he was ready for something different, even if it made him a bit melancholy.

Hunter looked up, blinking into the bright glare of the overcast day. As long as that something included Grace.

Grace, who had always been too good for him.

Grace, who he had missed more than he had realized.

Grace, who would kick his ass for telling her he would stay in Alaska one day and even thinking about the job offer the next.

When Grace made it clear she didn't love being a nomad, Hunter had been blindsided. She knew who he was and what he wanted. She knew Hunter wanted adventure. She knew he never said no. He figured she'd wanted that too. Why else would Grace have stuck with him this long?

So how the hell had he ended up on a rocky beach at the end of the world, actually contemplating turning down the opportunity of a lifetime?

He already knew the answer. Because he was getting a second chance with Grace. That was the true opportunity of a lifetime.

Hunter reached down his hand to pet Ruby, but his fingertips brushed the rocky soil instead. He had even gotten used to the damn dog. He loved that little furball.

He hung his head. Life had been easier when Grace had hated him.

Pushing himself up from the beach, Hunter decided now was as good a time as any for a cold beer. Maybe that would help him think.

He made his way back up Main Street. Hunter glanced at the coffee shop, trying to decide if guilt outweighed his thirst. But the double doors of the Buck beckoned to him like the gates of Heaven.

Hunter stepped into the restaurant. He hadn't been by yet today, and Grace didn't mind having time to herself. He would talk to her later, after the coffee shop had closed and if she wasn't too tired.

Hunter took a seat at the bar. It was halfway between lunch and dinner, and the Buck was nearly empty. "Can I get a pint, please?"

Wolfie pulled on the tap and passed the frosty glass to Hunter. "Anything else? Something to eat? Or want to tell me what's on your mind?"

Hunter took a long sip of the golden ale, smacking his lips. He was right. A beer did hit the spot. "How do you know anything is on my mind at all?"

Wolfie lifted a shoulder. "You don't have your laptop. You usually order coffee rather than a beer. And you're touchy."

Hunter let out a laugh. Wolfie had told him he'd been a psychologist before he moved from Germany to Alaska. He hadn't lost his touch for reading people, and the way he told the story, years behind the bar had only made him better at it. "You win. But it's nothing you can help with."

"Maybe not. But I can listen."

Hunter set down his glass. It wasn't Wolfie who was the problem. It was Hunter. He would have loved to talk it out. He needed someone to grab him by the shoulders and shake some sense into him before he made a huge mistake. Hunter had dedicated almost as many years to Grace as he had to his photography.

But only one would love him back. And it sucked that it was the same one who could leave him again.

The door swung open, and Wolfie looked up. "Ah. Never mind. The specialist has arrived."

He followed Wolfie's gaze. Natasha stood in the doorway, looking directly at Hunter. He shivered, remembering that night in the forest when she had scared the crap out of him. He hadn't crossed paths with Natasha since, and he was more than fine with that. Something about her put him on edge.

Hunter glanced back at Wolfie, dropping his voice a notch. "And what exactly makes her the specialist?"

Wolfie's mustache twitched. "Don't you know? Natasha is psychic. She has the sight."

"News to me." Hunter reached for his beer. Was Wolfie messing with him? Or was it just a small-town legend everyone bought into? Either way, it didn't make Hunter feel any less ridiculous that such an innocent-looking older woman gave him the creeps.

Despite Hunter's attempts to send her subliminal messages to sit somewhere else, Natasha walked over and hoisted her petite frame up onto the barstool next to him. Apparently, she wasn't so psychic after all.

She smiled, revealing a row of perfect pearly teeth. Though she was older than him, around Wolfie's age, maybe, his photographer's eye could see how beautiful she truly was. "A glass of champagne, please."

Wolfie set a flute glass in front of her, tipping a split of champagne over the top.

"Champagne?" Hunter eyed the bottle. "I didn't even know they served champagne here."

"They do, and it's delicious." She tipped her glass up, taking a sip. "Champagne always brings back good memories for me."

He shook his head. She might have the rest of the town fooled, but Hunter wasn't going to play along. He wasn't in the mood for games. "I'm not buying it."

"Not buying what?"

Hunter waved his hands. "This whole crazy-lady psychic act. I've met actual shamans. Mystics. Whatever you want to call them. I know the difference."

She gave him a patient smile. "You have me all figured out. Now, can we just sit here and have a normal conversation?"

Hunter hunched over the bar and drank his beer in silence while Natasha and Wolfie chatted. About the weather. How the town had changed. What it would be like this winter.

No woo-woo stuff. Nothing that gave Hunter the heebie-jeebies. Just like he thought. Nothing psychic about her.

Natasha turned to him suddenly. "So, are you going to take that job?"

Hunter choked on the last of his beer. He wiped his mouth on the back of his hand, trying to catch his breath.

Without so much as raising an eyebrow, Wolfie poured him another.

"What job?" Hunter asked.

Her blue eyes twinkled. "I'm not buying it."

He shifted on the barstool. Maybe Wolfie had been telling the truth about Natasha. If she wasn't psychic, she was a damn lucky guesser. "I don't know what I'm doing yet."

"You hear that?" She turned to Wolfie. "He's considering doing it."

Wolfie cocked an eyebrow. "Doing what?"

"Making a huge mistake." She finished her drink. "I better get going. See you next time."

Hunter narrowed his eyes. The comment had been directed at Wolfie. As if Hunter might not be here next time. "Natasha, wait. Which decision would be the mistake?"

She turned to look at him, her expression blank. "Why are you asking me a question you already know the answer to?"

And with that, she was gone.

Hunter's second beer suddenly looked much too small. "Lot of help she was."

Wolfie crossed his arms. "People make up a lot of stories about Natasha. Nothing mean necessarily. But the truth is scary. That's always been the problem."

"I could live with the truth. Not some fortune cookie garbage."

Wolfie quirked up the corner of his mouth. "Hey, you had your chance. You could've talked about it with me."

"Okay, fine. I'm in this deep. What would you do if you had to choose between a dream job and a dream woman?"

The barkeep smoothed his mustache. "Whatever you won't regret. Either set Grace free and live your life how you want or stay with Grace and change your life to make things work with her. Take it from someone who once waited too long to ask for what he wanted."

Two fishermen came in and sat at a booth by the window. Wolfie headed over to their table, leaving Hunter alone.

Staring into his beer, Hunter felt more confused than he had when he first got to Darling more than three weeks ago. It wasn't fair at all. He had come here trying to grieve for Jack. He hadn't expected to fall back in love with Grace. Or realize that he had never fallen out of love with her in the first place.

What an idiot he'd been. He hadn't come to Darling to get away from everything. He came here to be with the one person he loved most in this world.

Hunter had lost Aunt Linda. He had lost Jack. But he hadn't lost Grace. Not yet.

But if he wanted to be with her, he had to show her that he was serious. He had to make a sacrifice. Something to prove how much she meant to him. Something big.

Something like giving up his dream job.

His stomach twisted into a pretzel. This was going against his entire life philosophy. He never said no. But look where doing things the old way had gotten him? Successful and heartbroken. Maybe it was time for something different.

Why are you asking me a question you already know the answer to?

Goddammit. Maybe Natasha was psychic.

He checked the time. The Driftwood would be closing in an hour. As Wolfie walked by, Hunter signaled for one more beer. One more beer, and then he would go home and tell Grace about everything, including the job offer in New York. He'd put his heart into her hands.

The more he thought about it, the better he felt. Screw the job. Yes, it was a great opportunity. But they would replace him in a week if he walked away.

As far as the divorce, they could put a stop to that. As

long as Grace was in agreement, of course. Or get remarried. Hunter chuckled to himself. Wouldn't that be hilarious?

And when it came to photography, maybe he could scale back and take fewer trips. Or do something else. Dana could help him figure that out. She had already offered, and he knew he could count on her.

On that note, Hunter pulled out his phone. If Grace was the most important woman in his life, then Dana was the second. He had promised he would make a decision soon. Hunter owed her at least that much.

Taking a deep breath, Hunter clicked on his contacts, his thumb hovering over her name. Before he clicked the screen, the phone buzzed and the caller ID flashed Dana's name.

He almost fell off his barstool. She was calling *him*? Or was he that drunk from the home brew already? "Dana. I was just about to call you. Look, I decided—"

"Wait. Before you break my heart and say no, I want to apologize. I didn't mean to put pressure on you. I think running the whole show by myself, as much as I love it, has started to wear thin. Maybe I need a vacation too."

Hunter sat up. Dana, apologize? Things must be really bad. "Where do you want to go? I'll pay for it. No budget. Book whatever you need."

"Dang, I should've broken down a long time ago." Dana laughed. "Sorry. I'm feeling more emotional than Lauren and just as grouchy. Luckily, I haven't started vomiting or randomly falling asleep yet."

Goose bumps rose on Hunter's arms.

Grace had been exhausted every night for the past week. She had said it was from the coffee shop being so busy, but maybe it was more than that.

Her emotions were definitely all over the place. And she had lost her temper with him more than once, most recently this afternoon.

His mouth turned dry. Was there a chance Grace could be pregnant?

"Dana, I can't talk about the jobs right now. I'll explain everything later."

Hunter ended the call and pulled a few bills from his wallet, tucking them under his glass. He snuck out without saying goodbye to Wolfie, having learned the hard way that the old barkeep would refuse to take the money.

Hunter walked straight past the coffee shop and went to the store to ask Vivian for a favor.

He tiptoed around Grace and spent the rest of the day making plans for Saturday. This had to be special. The stuff of legends. Because Hunter was getting something people almost never got in life.

He was getting a second chance to do things right.

CHAPTER TWENTY-ONE

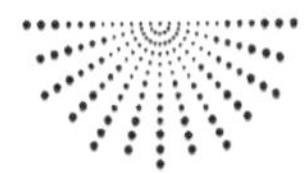

HUNTER

Hunter buttoned up his shirt, leaning closer to the mirror. He inspected the fine lines that crisscrossed his forehead and fanned out from the corners of his eyes. "You're getting old, Hart."

Too old to waste time.

Hunter was done fooling around. He wasn't twenty anymore. Life wasn't getting any longer. He knew what he wanted, and he didn't have time for doubt.

Ruby sat next to him, her blue gaze sincere.

He reached out and patted her head. "That's right, girl. We're going to be a family."

Hunter headed to the kitchen one more time to make sure everything was perfect.

Flowers? Check.

Candles? Check.

Sparkling water instead of wine? Check.

Hunter was lighting the candles when he heard footsteps on the stairs. He put the lighter back in the drawer and hurried out of the kitchen to greet Grace with a smile. "Welcome home."

She gave him a sideways glance. "Thanks?"

"How was work?"

Grace yawned into the back of her hand. "Another busy day. I can't remember the last time I was this exhausted."

Hunter smiled. He knew why she was tired.

"What's so funny?" Grace walked past him and into the kitchen. "Roses? And candles?"

He followed behind her. "I wanted to get you something special."

"Where did you get roses?" She leaned down to sniff the bouquet. "Better question. *Why* did you get roses?"

Hunter placed a hand on the small of her back and guided her to a chair. "Grace, honey. Why don't you sit down? I have something I want to talk to you about."

"Only if I get a glass of wine first."

"How about water?"

She frowned. "Water? No way. You realize there's a grocery store next door, right? I could fill the bathtub with wine if I wanted."

"Don't you think you should lay off the alcohol?"

Grace blinked at him. "You're going to have to spell this out for me."

His stomach fluttered as he took her hands in his. "Grace. I know it's probably too early to know for sure. But do you think there's any chance you could be pregnant?"

"Are you joking? That's not funny, Hunter. It's mean." Grace jerked her hands from his before stomping downstairs.

Hunter's heart squeezed. Clearly, she was terrified. Didn't she realize he was here for her? That he would do everything in his power to support her? She couldn't be worried he'd leave her now. He followed her, determined to finish the conversation. "Honey, please."

She had one hand on the door handle, her back to him. "If you need me, I'll be next door deciding between red and white."

"Let's talk to a doctor first. You're barely forty. It's still possible. I don't want to risk harming the baby."

Grace stiffened. "Hunter, I'm telling you. I'm not pregnant."

Hunter took another small step towards her. He longed to wrap her in a hug and promise her everything, but he didn't want to upset her even more, especially if she was pregnant. "If you're worried about raising this kid alone, don't be. I'm staying here. I'll be here for you. With you."

She turned towards him, her face stone. "I'm telling you the truth, Hunter. I'm not pregnant because I can't get pregnant. It's impossible."

"But we didn't—"

"No. It has nothing to do with birth control. After I turned thirty-seven, I went to a fertility clinic. They did a bunch of tests. My oven isn't really an oven. It's more of a cabinet. It's just there."

The blood drained from his face. That was the year that Grace had left him. For years, Hunter hadn't known what made her walk away, but he was starting to put the pieces together. "You what? But we weren't even trying for a baby!"

She stuck her chin out. "But I knew I wanted one. With or without you. I wasn't going to wait anymore."

His body went numb. Who was this stranger? He and Grace had always shared everything with each other. At one point, he had known her better than he had known himself. Or so he thought. Apparently, he had been wrong about that, along with so many other things. "Why didn't you tell me?"

"I'm telling you right now."

Hunter swayed on his feet, dizzy with anger and grief. His body turned hot, and for a moment, he thought he might be sick. "No. Why didn't you tell me back then? I know I screwed up, and I have lived with that guilt since you've been gone, Grace. Your dreams should've been as important to me as my own. I should've made them a priority from the beginning, and I feel horrible that I didn't. Especially a family. I thought we ran out of time, that I took something you could never get back. Now I find it was never even a possibility in the first place? That's torn me apart! It tore our marriage apart!"

Her face flushed as her voice grew louder. "Are you kidding me right now? I'm the one who should be upset here! A husband who didn't care. Doesn't care. If you think that not having kids is why our marriage failed, then you're more oblivious than I thought."

Hunter gaped at her. She couldn't actually believe that. He might have only been in Darling for three weeks, but they had almost twenty years of history between them. That had to count for something. "You really think I don't care?"

Her gaze was colder than the sea that surrounded the island. "You do what works for you. Always have. Always will. You're the one who tore our marriage apart, Hunter. Not me."

He wanted to rip his hair out. He wanted to scream and stomp his feet like a child. He had tried to do the right thing tonight, and it had backfired horribly. He was out of ideas and full of shock. "Just tell me what to do, Grace. Tell me the answer."

She was quiet for a moment. Hunter held his breath. Whatever she asked, he'd do it. He'd do anything he could if there was a snowball's chance in hell he could make this right. "I think you should take that job in Sedona. Give us some space."

His stomach sank. Not only did she not believe he cared, she didn't even want him there. "That's really what you want? What about your birthday? It's in three days."

"You'll either be back or you won't. But we need time to cool off. Or maybe you don't. But I do." Grace shook her head, her voice shaky. "It's just too much, too fast. What happened with Jack. Living together again. This isn't the time to make big decisions. Neither of us are thinking straight."

Hunter swallowed, his throat thick. It wasn't that he didn't want to give her time. It was that they didn't have it. He had been so wrapped up in the possibility of Grace being pregnant that he hadn't talked to her about not getting divorced yet. And with only a week to go until it was finalized, there didn't seem to be much to talk about. "I'll see if Mac can fly me out tomorrow. That way, I can be back in time for your birthday."

"Maybe."

He set his jaw. Not maybe. He had to. He wasn't giving up yet. Hunter had staked everything on this. He was all in. He hadn't exactly turned down the creative director job, but he hadn't taken it either.

His head throbbed. Hunter still hadn't had a chance to talk to Grace about that either. He had planned to tonight, along with discussing the divorce. But none of this was going according to plan.

Hunter went upstairs, and Ruby followed behind him. After he blew out the candles one by one, he called Wolfie and got Mac's number. Luckily, Hunter was able to get a flight out first thing the next morning.

In a daze, he made quick work of filling his small suitcase and shoving his laptop into his backpack. Ruby sat in his room, watching him with her crystal eyes. He'd miss that little dog.

A great sense of loss crept over him as he tried to imagine life away from Grace and everything, and everyone, he had come to care for in Darling.

Hunter took a deep breath. It was just for a few days, not forever. But he couldn't shake the feeling that this was the end.

A sob clawed at his chest, but Hunter willed himself not to cry. He had told Grace everything. He had put his heart on the line. But she hadn't returned the favor.

Would it be different if they had more time? But Hunter had almost two decades of time, and he had still managed to screw it up. Why did he think it would be any different now?

Why are you asking me a question you already know the answer to?

Because, just this once, Hunter wanted the answer to be different.

CHAPTER TWENTY-TWO

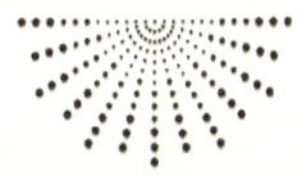

GRACE

"Are you sure?" Vivian's green eyes rounded with apparent concern.

"Totally." Grace gave a firm nod. "We're still having the party."

"But Hunter—"

"Will be back in time, or he won't. I've survived this long without him, haven't I?" Grace left out the part where Hunter had promised to be there. Mostly because she didn't know if she could stand to be disappointed one more time.

"Oh," Vivian said.

Oh.

Exactly. Grace didn't have the words either. Their fight still hung over her head. No matter how many times she replayed it in her mind, no matter how much she wished she had said this or done that, it didn't change what had actually happened.

Grace stared at her chamomile tea, which had gone cold

thirty minutes ago. Despite everything, an ember of hope still burned inside her heart. Grace hated herself for holding her breath every time the bell over the door chimed. It was never Hunter, of course. Apparently, she used up her quota of miracles when he showed up the first time.

She should know better. In romance books, a grand entrance only happened once in a story. Grace had already had hers.

Besides, wasn't this what she had wanted in the first place? For Hunter to go away? She had her space back. She should be popping champagne, not trying not to cry while she pulled shots of espresso.

Pathetic.

Grace had shed enough tears for her husband. Anyway, she wasn't sad. She was angry. Angry at herself for believing things could ever be different. For being stupid enough to fall back in love with him.

She fiddled with her tea bag. It was better that he left. Good riddance. The safest place for Hunter to be was on the other side of the world. Then maybe she could get her head on straight, and life could get back to normal.

I want to be there when you realize normal isn't what you want at all.

Her heart squeezed. Who the hell was he to tell her what she wanted? She didn't even know that herself.

"The party will still be fun." Vivian gave her a reassuring smile.

Grace forced a small smile in return. "I'm excited for it."

If only she could lie to herself so easily.

Tomorrow was her birthday, with or without Hunter. And after all the trouble Vivian had gone through to help put everything together, canceling the party wasn't an option.

Besides, everyone Grace had talked to about the party

had said they were looking forward to it. She could at least power through for their sake. The town had given her so much, after all.

Ruby whined.

"I've got to take her out." Grace stood from the bistro table and carried her cup over to the sink, pouring out her cold tea. "Is there anything I need to do to help tomorrow?"

Vivian finished the last of her green tea, adding her empty mug to the dish bin. "Are you kidding? It's your birthday. I would've loved to do a surprise party for you, but you know this town can't keep a secret."

Grace shuddered. "Thank goodness. I hate surprises."

For some reason, they always seemed to be bad.

Vivian headed back to her place, and Grace's shoulders sagged. She had plenty of work to do, as usual. But it all seemed so overwhelming. Taking Ruby outside seemed like the best place to start.

After clipping on Ruby's leash, the two of them walked down to the beach. Despite being early summer, the weather remained as gloomy as Grace's mood. The clouds were dark and heavy, the air damp with the promise of rain.

Letting Ruby off the leash, Grace looked out at the blue-black water. Had it only been a month ago that she stood here thinking how perfect life was?

She blew air through her lips. Ignorance really was bliss.

Grace blamed it on Hunter. He had shown her she was wrong. He had shown her it could be so much better.

The constant mist that blanketed Darling morphed into fat raindrops, landing on Grace's hood with a smack. She stood there in the downpour, the world turning blurry around her.

Ruby ran up, her normally fluffy fur plastered to her body.

Grace sighed. The entire apartment was going to smell like a wet dog. "Come on, you scoundrel. It's going to take half an hour to get you dry."

The two of them made their way back to the coffee shop.

Unlocking the door, Grace realized the next time they did this after-work routine, she would be forty.

She didn't feel forty in her mind. Maybe no one did. She still felt nineteen, with all of her own dreams. Like an idiot, she still felt hopeful about life. Or she used to, anyway.

If one thing was certain, it was that Grace was going into her forties firmly single. The dating app had been a bust. The divorce would be finalized in less than a week.

At least she hadn't screwed that up. Putting off calling the attorney that day had worked out for the best. Because while Grace still had so many unanswered questions, it was clear that she and Hunter didn't belong together. They wanted different things, and being together meant one of them was destined to be unhappy.

So that was her birthday gift to herself. Not love, but the confirmation that her ideas about love had been right all this time. It was a crock of shit. A dangerous, unforgiving, unpredictable crock of shit. She'd rather sit at home with her dog and read.

As she toweled off Ruby, someone knocked on the coffee shop door. Grace looked up to see a blue raincoat peeking in the window.

She opened the door. "Elle? Did you need something?"

Elle gave her a cautious smile. "Sorry to bother you. I'm sure you had a long day, and you'll have an even longer one tomorrow with the party and everything. But Mac just got back from Juneau." She pulled a package out of a plastic bag and handed it to Grace. "Someone overnighted this to you. I tried to keep it dry."

Grace stared at the familiar handwriting on the label. "Hunter."

"That was nice of him to send you a birthday present."

Grace's chest tightened. It was the nicest thing that could be said about this situation. "He had to leave for a work thing last minute."

Elle cleared her throat. "If you want to talk, I'm here."

Grace forced a smile. "Thanks, but I'm fine. He told me he probably wouldn't make it back by tomorrow."

Liar.

Elle's face relaxed. "Okay, great. Then I worried about nothing."

Grace knit her brows together. The two of them would chat when Elle came into the Driftwood every so often, but Grace had never thought they were particularly close. Elle was basically famous and probably had a ton of friends. Grace assumed she didn't even register on Elle's radar. "You worried? About me?"

"Of course. Matters of the heart can be tricky. Especially because men are idiots."

Grace laughed and thanked Elle again as she left. Maybe they were more like friends than Grace had realized.

She turned the package over in her hand. Ruby stared up at her with crystal-blue eyes. "Should I open it?"

She took Ruby's silence as a yes.

Grabbing a knife, Grace carefully opened the package and pulled out a wrapped box. A letter tumbled out onto the floor. She reached for it, unfolding the paper.

To the love of my life—

Sorry to miss your birthday. I hope you like this, but I get if you want to smash it against the wall. I have my own copy in case you (understandably) choose to trash this one.

I stand by what I said, Grace. I couldn't have done any of this without you, and now that I have had a taste of what it's like, I don't want to.

We had a good life. We've seen the world twice over. I have an incredible career. But none of that compares to getting to be your husband, and I want you to know that. I want the world to know that.

I have the opportunity for a new job. I'd still have to travel, but just to New York City. I could make regular visits to Darling. I'd be working as a creative director for a magazine, and this letter, this photo, would be printed in my first issue as my introduction to the readers. I want the world to know what I should've been shouting from the rooftops a long time ago.

That you're my everything. That I should've given you everything you ever wanted, especially because I didn't need a damn thing. Having you was more than enough.

I know it's your birthday, and it's selfish for me to ask for a gift from you. But if you give me one more chance, I won't screw it up. What do you think? If I take the job, would we have a chance?

Love you forever and always,

Hunter

Grace didn't realize she was crying until a tear blurred the ink of his signature.

She wiped at her face. It was stupid to cry now. She had already done that so much, and it hadn't changed a thing.

Grace set the card aside and ripped open the box. The wrapping paper was the same pink color as the dress she had bought for her birthday. Hunter had never seen the dress, and now he definitely wouldn't. How had he known?

She sucked in a shaky breath. Because he knew her better than anyone, of course. Probably even better than she knew herself.

Grace lifted the framed photo from the box. The picture of her and Hunter at the beach stared back at her.

Her eyes burned. How dare he? How dare he be so

wonderful and remind her how much she loved him? How dare he give her everything and then disappear?

But the gift made the truth obvious. Hunter wouldn't be back in time. He broke his promise and would miss her birthday.

Her heart hiccupped. But he planned to tell the world how much he loved her.

The creative director job would be just about perfect. He would get to do what he loved, and Grace would get the best of both worlds. She could have both Hunter and her life here.

Except it was past time to accept that the chapter of her life that included Hunter was over. As much as she loved having him here, look how quickly they had caused each other pain? And what if he did want kids? Or got bored of Darling? Each unknown led Grace to the same conclusion.

She couldn't gamble her heart anymore.

Grace lifted her head, taking in the coffee shop. She had gotten her tiny little world back. It was what she had wanted. Except it didn't feel cozy and safe anymore. It felt like a giant gaping hole. Everywhere she looked, she only saw everything she had lost.

Ruby nuzzled Grace's leg. She reached down to scratch her ears, wet-dog smell and all.

Grace swallowed, but the lump in her throat refused to move. "Let's hope forty is better."

* * *

"Happy birthday, Grace." Wolfie leaned in to give her a hug. "You look fantastic."

"I'll say." Charlotte, Wolfie's wife and co-owner of the Buck, ushered Grace inside the restaurant. "A real heart-breaker."

Grace smiled, hoping it was convincing. If only they knew that she was the one whose heart had been broken.

Vivian's eyes lit up when she saw Grace. "You look amazing."

Grace wrapped her friend in a tight hug. "Thank you. I really mean thank *you* because I never would've gotten this dress without you."

It had almost killed Grace to put it on, though. She had imagined Hunter's reaction when he saw her in it, wearing it as she danced the night away with him. She hadn't imagined that she'd be here without him.

Her chest constricted. Just like she wanted.

Vivian stepped back and nodded in the direction of the bar. "Champagne?"

"Lots, please." What better way to forget her troubles than to drown them in bubbles?

As they made their way through the crowd, almost everyone stopped them to wish Grace a happy birthday, punctuated by the sparkly *HAPPY BIRTHDAY, GRACE* banner that Vivian had strung across the doorway.

Grace's shoulders tensed, despite the smile frozen on her face. She hated being the center of attention. But everyone looked so happy. Just because she was miserable wasn't a reason to ruin their fun.

When they finally reached the bar, Vivian handed Grace a glass of champagne. "So…"

"He's not back. I don't know when or if he'll be back."

Vivian's face fell. "Oh God. I'm sorry I asked."

"It's fine, really." Grace took a sip of champagne. Hopefully, that would soften the lump in her throat. "He sent a gift, though."

Vivian peered at her. "Are you okay?"

Grace forced a smile. She refused to let Vivian think she

wasn't enjoying the celebration. "I'm great. I'm glad this happened now. My forties can be a fresh start."

"That'd be easier to believe if you didn't look like you were about to cry."

Her eyes burned, and Grace blinked furiously. The last thing she wanted was to have a breakdown at her own birthday. "No, I don't."

Vivian gave her arm a reassuring squeeze. "Come on. Let's have fun. I'll keep drinks in your hand, and no one will ask about Hunter. If they do, I'll create a distraction by doing some interpretative dancing. Trust me, no one will be thinking about your love life after that."

Grace let out a strangled laugh and took another gulp of champagne. She could totally do this, especially with a friend like Vivian by her side. "Fun. I can do that. Who cares if Hunter isn't here?"

You do, you idiot, her heart whispered.

Shut up, heart. Useless thing. Worse than useless. A torture device.

She drained her glass and reached for another. "Let's get this party started!"

Grace danced, ate a huge slice of cake, and drank way too much champagne. She laughed and talked until she almost lost her voice. The party went late into the night until even the sun needed rest and disappeared for a few hours.

It was the performance of a lifetime.

Vivian helped Grace back to her apartment. After asking three times if she'd be okay, Vivian went home with a promise to check in tomorrow.

"Great party," Grace called out after her, her voice as scratchy as sandpaper.

Ruby yipped and spun in circles as soon as Grace was inside the door, probably just as excited for a bathroom break as she was to see her.

"Let's go." Grace let the dog outside without a leash. It was the wee hours, and hardly anyone was out. Most of the town was probably sleeping off the party.

Ruby stayed close as they walked to the water. Once they reached the beach, Grace pulled off her flats and let out a moan as the rocky shore massaged her feet.

She had never been at the beach this time of night. It was eerily quiet, the only sound the soft lapping waves. There were no cars driving by, no people, no birds. There was just enough light to see the water, as if someone had dimmed the lights in a theater.

It was so beautiful that it broke her heart.

Grace plopped to the ground, sitting right on the rocks. Her dress tore with a loud rip, and she fingered the split in the fabric.

Her throat tightened. Did everything beautiful have to end?

Ruby walked up and lay down next to her. Grace scratched the dog's ears. "So, that's how it's going to be, huh? We're going to sleep on the beach tonight like a couple of wild animals? I haven't done the outdoors thing in years, Ruby. I think I'm too old for that now."

Her mind wandered to Hunter. Was he still in Sedona? Or had he already moved on to the next job? Despite what his letter had said, work was the real love of his life. Otherwise, he would have been there tonight.

She closed her eyes. Grace had blamed him for everything. What killed her was realizing she was just as guilty. She should've told him about her fertility testing. She should've told him everything about wanting a home. She should've fought for what she wanted and fought for him.

And with Hunter gone and only five days until the divorce was finalized, Grace doubted she'd ever get a chance to plead her case.

Her breath hitched, and she opened her eyes. She had to make a choice. She had thought she had left Hunter in the past two years ago, but she was wrong. She had kept a spot in her heart for him, one that she willingly let him back into the minute he showed up.

Her desperation at getting him to leave was suddenly so clear. It wasn't that she didn't love Hunter anymore. It was that she loved him too much.

Which was worse? To close her heart to him forever? Or to torture herself by believing things could be different?

Grace dusted off her feet and slipped on her shoes again. She gathered up Ruby, holding her close as she trudged across the beach towards home.

Once inside the cozy apartment, Grace walked to her bedside table and pulled out the photo of her and Hunter on the beach. She stared at it, begging the tiny little Grace in the picture to tell her what to do.

Hunter insisted he always told her the truth. And maybe he had. Maybe Grace was the one who had lied to herself.

Maybe her fortieth birthday gift to herself would be finally moving on.

Grace wandered to the guest room, just like she had every night since Hunter had left. She took in the neatly made bed. She opened the empty dresser drawers, her spirits sinking lower with each one. His musky scent tickled her memories. One day, it would disappear altogether. She couldn't wait, and she dreaded it.

Grace closed the door behind her as she left the room. She needed to get a grip. She would die of embarrassment if anyone ever found out. He wasn't dead, after all.

After unzipping her ruined dress, Grace pulled on sweats and curled up in her bed. Who gave a damn about showering? There was no one there to care. She was alone.

Just like she wanted.

Grace patted the quilt, and Ruby jumped up to join her. She pulled the dog close.

Tears rolled down her cheeks, disappearing into Ruby's fur. Hunter wasn't the idiot. Grace was.

She had fallen for him again, and that asshole broke her heart.

There wasn't enough champagne in the world to help her forget Hunter Hart.

CHAPTER TWENTY-THREE

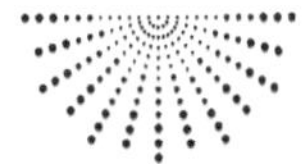

GRACE

Grace checked the time. Five minutes to two. "You want to get a drink?"

Vivian arched an eyebrow. "At the Buck?"

"It's either that or my living room. I need to get out of here." Grace clasped her hands together. "Please?"

Vivian blew air through her lips. "Okay. But just one."

She helped tidy up the cafe, wiping down tables while Grace cleaned the equipment and restocked. As Grace counted the till, Vivian took Ruby out for a bathroom break.

Recording the tally for the day, Grace eyed the tip jar. She hadn't even had a tip jar at first. The whole thing made her uncomfortable. But the town, in its typical way, would just leave money on the counter or shove it into a clean cup.

Grace fished out a handful of bills. That money was supposed to be her emergency fund. But didn't a broken heart count?

The door chimed as Vivian and Ruby got back. Grace pulled a sweater overhead and flicked off the lights. "Ready?"

With a groan, Vivian followed her across the street to the Buck.

Once they passed through the double doors, Grace made a beeline for the bar. She normally preferred a booth, but she wasn't here to eat. It had been at least a decade since she had tried to fix her feelings with alcohol. It had never worked before, but try, try again.

Grace hopped on a barstool, patting the one next to her. Vivian looked at the thing like it was covered in spikes.

"Come on." Grace hooked her foot around the bottom of the stool and scooted it out an inch. "It's just like getting on a horse. Or a bicycle. Whatever."

Vivian perched stiffly on the seat. "Are you sure you haven't been drinking already?"

Grace laughed. "I haven't, and that's the problem. What are you having?"

"Water? I think I might still be recovering from your birthday party."

"That was two days ago." Grace rested her elbows on the countertop, inspecting the various bottles that lined the back of the bar. "So, does that mean champagne is off the table?"

Vivian turned the color of seaweed. "Talk to me next year."

Grace caught Wolfie's eye. "Two margaritas, please."

"Finally, a challenge." He mixed the cocktails and set the drinks in front of them with a wink. "Pouring beer all day gets boring."

Grace licked the salted rim and took a sip, puckering her mouth at the twang of fresh lime juice. "It doesn't get better than this."

"I'll take your word for it." Vivian eyed her drink warily. It seemed to be as suspect as the barstool. "Want mine too?"

Grace gawked at her. "You can't tell me you've never had a margarita."

"Have we met?" Vivian reached for her drink, nudging the salt to the side with her finger. She took a tentative sip, and her eyes widened. "Holy cow. Never mind, I'm keeping this one."

Grace chuckled. "See? Who needs men? This is way more fun without Hunter."

"That would be more believable if you didn't specifically name him."

Grace bit the inside of her cheek. Dammit. Stupid brain. She was over Hunter. So totally over him. "It's the tequila talking."

"You still haven't heard from him, huh?"

Grace shifted in her seat. The mix of alcohol and too many feelings was a slippery slope.

No, she hadn't heard from him, and Hunter's silence sent a stronger message than words ever could.

His feelings had changed. Or maybe this was how he'd always felt, but he had been confused by his grief when he first got there. Now that he had a clear head, he'd realized the same thing that Grace did. They had tried being together, and it didn't work. "Not so much as a peep. But enough about Hunter. That's old news."

"What about trying the dating app thing again?"

Grace cringed. "Hell no. I think I am going to be single forever. Which I'm totally fine with. What did being in a relationship ever do for me? Drag me around the world? Take the best years of my life?"

Vivian pressed her lips together, stirring her drink with the tiny cocktail straw.

Grace sighed. "Okay. Let's hear it."

"It just doesn't seem like you're over him. I think you still love him. And he still loves you."

"What do you even know about love?" Grace snapped. Vivian paled, and Grace instantly wished she could take her words back. Her bruises were still tender, and nothing hit harder than the truth. But that did not make it okay to bite her friend's head off. "I'm sorry. I shouldn't have said that."

Vivian's green eyes glistened. "The only thing you shouldn't do is hold yourself back. If you love Hunter, don't wait for that magical day when it's going to be the right situation. It's never the right time. Never the right place. Real life isn't like a book."

Grace swallowed, her throat tight. Vivian was right. People could die of old age waiting for the perfect circumstances. But there was no changing the past. The best Grace could do was to make use of the time she had now. Starting with focusing on enjoying the life she had created for herself in Darling. "I think I need another margarita."

"I'll have one with you." Vivian offered her a small smile, apparently accepting the peace offering.

The jukebox kicked on, and the clinking of silverware and din of conversation faded away as Grace remembered the night she and Hunter had danced together. She shivered, suddenly needing something stronger than a margarita. "How about a tequila shot?"

Vivian gagged. "No way."

Grace couldn't help but laugh. "When did you get so wise?"

"Just born that way, I guess."

Grace didn't push Vivian, even though she suspected there was more to the story. No one was born like that. Vivian had the kind of wisdom that came from learning things the hard way. Something had happened. Something Vivian kept to herself. "What's new with you? I feel like we've talked about me nonstop lately."

Vivian shrugged. "That's because you're the only one with anything interesting going on. You've heard about one day in my life, you've heard about them all."

"I hear Charlotte's cousin is visiting again."

Vivian's cheeks turned red. "So what?"

"You like him." Grace wiggled her finger.

"He's alright."

Charlotte's cousin was around Vivian's age and the definition of tall, dark, and handsome. "From what I remember, he's much better than alright."

"Hey. I thought you were married to Hunter."

Grace kept the smile frozen on her face, even if the reminder of her marriage made the margarita climb back up her throat. "About to be divorced, remember? In four short days. And I have eyes."

"Yeah, well, it doesn't matter. He's not my type."

Grace gently bumped her friend's shoulder. "Alright, then, I gotta know. What is your type?"

Vivian's face turned sourer than if she had been sipping on a glass of pure lime juice. "No one is my type."

"In that case, you could do worse than Charlotte's cousin."

"Nope. Too handsome. Too rich. Too stuck-up."

"Two of three isn't bad." Grace winked. "You never know. Love works in mysterious ways."

"Excuse me, we're here to have a good time without men, remember?"

"In that case, what's left to talk about?"

Vivian stuck out her bottom lip. "In this town? Nothing."

Grace barked a laugh. "We both need a vacation."

"*You* need a vacation. I told you I would dog-sit anytime you wanted."

The idea of going away for a bit was tempting. Grace hadn't left Alaska since she had first arrived. The problem was that she had been all over the world with Hunter. The entire planet held memories of him. Darling was the only place that was just hers. Until it wasn't.

Everywhere she looked, she thought of Hunter. At this

rate, she'd have to go to Mars if she wanted a place without memories. But he probably had a photoshoot planned there already. "Maybe you're right."

"Now is the time to do it. Less chance of bad weather this time of year."

Grace wrinkled her forehead. She hadn't thought about that. "What if there's a freak storm and I can't get back for a long time and go out of business?"

"I know where you keep the spare key. I'm sure making espresso isn't that hard."

Grace shook her head. "Does everyone know where I keep the spare key?"

"What we all want to know is why you even bother to lock the door."

Grace finished her drink, the ice clinking as she set down the glass. "I'll never get over this place."

"We all hope you never do." Vivian slid off her stool and offered Grace her arm. "But for now, I think it's time to call it a day. I want to go home while I can still walk without zigzagging all over the street."

They each left a bill on the counter, walking out of the Buck and across the street. Vivian hiccupped. "You got it from here?"

Grace fumbled with her key. "Almost."

"See, if you didn't lock the door, this wouldn't be a problem."

Grace chuckled as she unlocked the door. "Good night. I'll see you tomorrow."

Vivian went home, and Grace stepped inside the coffee shop.

Ruby wiggled, excited to see her as always.

After filling Ruby's bowl with kibble, Grace poured herself a large glass of water. She was going to feel those margaritas in the morning. If there was one thing that objectively sucked about getting older, it had to be the hangovers.

Grace remembered a perfect summer night in San Diego when she and Hunter had drunk two pitchers of margaritas. Sure, they felt like hell the next morning, but they had been young and happy and in love, and it had been worth it.

It had all been worth it.

She rubbed her forehead. Maybe it was the tequila or the emotional stress or her conversation with Vivian, but Grace asked herself the first honest question she had in years. Not why she had stayed with Hunter so long. Not why he hadn't been a better husband.

But why she didn't let herself be happy? Why didn't she live the life she wanted, knowing full well that Hunter would've supported her every step of the way?

He had offered her the world, and Grace had been too afraid to take it.

Grace wrapped her arms around herself, suddenly chilled. She had spent the past two years telling herself that Hunter was the villain. But what if Grace was her own worst enemy?

CHAPTER TWENTY-FOUR

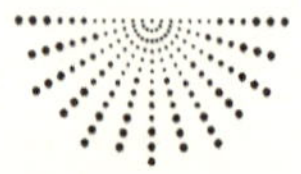

HUNTER

Three days.

Three days until he would be divorced from Grace.

Three days until his world came crashing down, once and for all.

Hunter took a deep breath, resisting the urge to bash his camera against one of the iconic red rocks. Despite being in one of the most jaw-dropping locations on Earth, he couldn't take a photo to save his life. The problem had nothing to do with his photography skills. Hunter had been struggling ever since he had left Darling.

He should've never walked away from Grace. He didn't want to. But she had needed space, and he had needed to officially tell Jack goodbye. Hunter suspected that Dana had arranged the job in Sedona on purpose as a way to give him closure. Grace had seen right through it too. What better place to honor Jack's life than in his hometown?

But Hunter had royally screwed up when he hadn't made it back in time for Grace's birthday. It was one thing to give her space when she asked for it. It was another not to keep a promise, especially after spending the last month trying to prove he could do just that.

The plan had been to give Grace a couple of days to cool off, go back to Alaska, and celebrate her birthday together. But one day turned into two. Then three, and now four.

The more time that spread between where he was now and when he had left, the harder it was to say the words that should be so easy.

Hunter wasn't upset that Grace hadn't told him about the fertility testing when it happened. He wasn't even upset about not being able to have children with her.

He was upset that she had carried that by herself all this time. She hadn't even trusted him enough to support her as she went through that.

Grace had always wanted kids, and Hunter wanted her to have everything that her heart desired. But the only thing his heart desired was her.

He tried to explain all that in his letter. According to the tracking number, the package had been delivered. Hunter had thought Grace might call after she read it or at least send him a pissed-off text. But there had been nothing but silence, which must mean she hated him as much as she had said. That killed him.

The muse had also left Hunter, deciding it would rather stay in Darling with Grace. A fitting punishment. Or maybe that was the great irony. Grace had been the muse all these years. He had always loved photography. But being in Alaska with Grace brought him back to those early days when he had taken pictures because he wanted to, not just because someone paid for them.

It had occurred to Hunter, briefly, to give it all up. Give it up and take the creative director job. Trade in fieldwork for a desk job and a regular schedule. He loved his art, and some days, it felt like the only thing he was capable of doing right. But the same career that had given him so much also took from him.

He and Grace had lived a thousand adventures, thanks to his work. The kind of adventures most people only dreamed about. But it had also torn them apart. Even now, it kept him from the one place that he tried to convince himself he didn't want to be.

Jack had to be rolling in his grave. Or whatever the phrase was when someone was cremated and spread amongst the red rocks of Sedona. He'd be asking Hunter what the hell he was doing here when he should be in Darling, fighting for Grace with everything he had.

But it was pointless. Even if Hunter and Grace were in the same room, it wouldn't change the fact that there were a million miles between them. A million unspoken words. A million regrets.

Running a hand through his hair, Hunter picked up the camera to try again. He told himself that this wasn't the red rocks of Sedona, but rather, it was the thick trees and rocky beaches of Alaska. He wasn't taking pictures of towering formations but taking pictures of Grace. He could see Ruby sitting patiently by his side. He could taste one of Wolfie's cold beers waiting for him at the end of the day. Hunter could feel the constant mist chilling his fingers and gathering on his rain jacket.

Just like that, he was in the zone. He felt the shot. It was like he couldn't take enough photos. After a couple of hours and catching the last good bit of light, Hunter finally called it a day.

He trudged back to the hotel, relieved the outing hadn't been a total waste. Even though Hunter had struggled to get into the flow, there was something peaceful about this place. Maybe it was the fact that it was time to let Jack go. He would always hold his friend in his heart, but Hunter couldn't stop living altogether either. He had Grace to thank for that. Hunter wouldn't be ready to move on by now if she hadn't helped him through his grief.

Hunter smiled to himself. He would love to tell Grace about today. To thank her. Maybe that would help her understand how much he cared about her, that she was a critical piece to his soul.

Or maybe she wouldn't even answer the phone.

He kicked at a rock, stirring up a cloud of rust-colored dirt. Hunter choked on the dust and bent over, trying to catch his breath on the other side of a coughing fit. What a dumbass.

If that didn't sum it up. He'd always been his own worst enemy. The good news was there was no one left to care.

Well. Almost no one.

Back at the hotel, Dana sat on the patio of the bar, drinking a margarita. The salt slid down the glass as condensation gathered in the early summer heat.

Hunter's mouth watered. He had been trying to avoid alcohol. Between his memories of Jack and what happened with Grace, it was almost guaranteed he'd wake up with a hangover once he started drinking.

"Want one?" Dana grinned, her eyes hidden behind massive sunglasses.

Hunter slumped into a chair. Dana never joined him on shoots. He didn't know why she insisted on coming along for this one, especially when he didn't want to be around anyone right now. "Why are you even here?"

"Maybe I came to experience the vortexes." She tapped her nails on the table. "Does it even matter? Half of LA is in Sedona these days. Or at least it seems that way based on real estate prices."

"The vortexes," Hunter muttered, ordering a margarita

when the server came back. Good intentions and all that. It was quickly delivered, along with chips and salsa.

The first sip had a bite to it, the liquor float on top making him wince before filling his belly with warmth. Dangerous, just like he had thought.

Dana sighed. "Look, I'm worried about you. How long have we been working together?"

Hunter used a warm chip to scoop up chunky salsa. He and Dana had been a team for almost ten years. Their careers had taken off together. She had spotted Hunter when he had yet to make a dime from his photos. He was one of her first clients, and the rest was history.

Other managers had tried to lure him away over the years, more interested in their potential commission check than his art. Hunter had never once been tempted to leave Dana. She was family. "Forever. What does that have to do with anything?"

The sun dipped behind the hotel, casting long shadows. But the heat of the day clung on. Dana pushed back her sunglasses, resting them on her head. "Something is different. You've never disappeared for a month before. The camera is usually part of your arm. What is really going on? Is there something you aren't telling me?"

Hunter drained half of his drink. He didn't feel a thing. Should've ordered a pitcher. The thought reminded him of that weekend in San Diego with Grace, and his heart squeezed. It was impossible to get away from the memories when she was as much a part of him as his photography. "I don't know."

"You know." Dana's brown gaze held his. "What happened in Alaska? Come on, kid. If you can't tell me, who can you tell? You're really SOL."

His throat grew thick. Dana had been there with him through everything. Through losing people he loved.

Through his career skyrocketing and having to adjust to real fame and wealth. Through struggling between what he wanted to do with his art and what others wanted him to do. There was only one thing to tell her. The truth.

Hunter told her about Grace. About the divorce papers. About falling back in love, or maybe remembering he had been in love all this time, just to screw it all up again. "So that's it. I'm right back where I started."

"That really sucks. And there's nothing you can do?" As usual, Dana didn't mince words.

Hunter shook his head. "I have gone over it a thousand times, looking for one thing I could've done differently. Grace made it clear she's not happy with me."

"You know what makes a great story? Surprise."

Hunter picked up his glass and focused on the lime wheel bobbing on top. "What are you saying?"

"What I am saying is you should do the last thing anyone expects. Go back."

He rubbed the back of his neck. It was exactly what he wanted to do if he didn't think it would blow up in his face. "What's the point? I already know how the story ends with me and Grace. Not well. Most likely with me facedown in a pitcher of beer."

"I'm not promising it's going to work out. But at least you'll know. My guess is if you're feeling this way, she might be too."

Hunter leaned his head back to take in the sunset streaking across the sky, but he didn't find the answers there either. He looked back at Dana. "And if it goes horribly? If she tells me to get the hell out and go screw myself? If she does actually hate me, and what little I have left of my heart gets stomped on once and for all?"

"Then you're still ahead. You don't have to wonder anymore." Dana gave him a mischievous smile. "And if it works out, that creative director job might be the perfect fit for you and Grace."

He let out a huff. "You never miss a chance to take your shot, do you?"

"How else are you supposed to score?"

Hunter took a deep breath. Dana was a shark, a bulldog. She wasn't a touchy-feely kind of person. But she also knew him better than almost anyone. What if she was right?

His brain kept insisting that he knew how the story ended. That there was no point in torturing himself. But his heart asked a question that was impossible to ignore.

Didn't he have every reason in the world to still try? It sure as hell beat spending the rest of his life wondering if things could've been different.

Why are you asking me a question you already know the answer to?

His breath caught. Hunter might have no idea what Grace wanted right now, but there was one thing he knew for sure. He hadn't lost hope that things could be different. Not just different. Better.

Hunter pushed away his half-finished drink as he stood. He leaned across the table to kiss Dana on the cheek. "Please clear my schedule."

"It's cleared. I'll text you the details of your flight."

"You're the best."

"Likewise." She smiled, lifting her glass. "It's why we make such a great team. Besides, I'm just relieved I don't have to hear you mope about this forever. It was getting me down."

Hunter laughed. "No mercy, huh?"

"Never. Someone has to kick your butt once in a while." She jerked a thumb in the direction of the hotel. "Now, get going."

Deciding he had wasted enough time, he jogged back to

his room and threw his clothes into his suitcase. He had just finished packing up his gear when his phone buzzed.

True to her word, Dana had booked him a flight. She was the least likely fairy godmother in the world. But he couldn't imagine anyone better for the job.

Hunter checked out of the hotel, started up the rental car, and headed back to the Phoenix airport.

He was going home.

CHAPTER TWENTY-FIVE

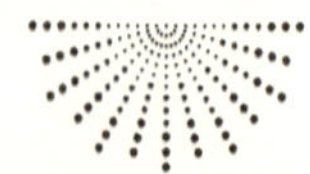

GRACE

Three days.

Three days until Grace would be officially unmarried to Hunter Hart.

Three days until the last thread between them would be snipped into two.

She should be happy. Thrilled. Tap-dancing around the coffee shop in unadulterated joy and flinging confetti into the air. Grace had been done with that relationship for a long time. Ever since Hunter arrived in Darling, she had been holding her breath for him to leave, just like she knew he would.

But had Grace wanted him to prove her right? Or wrong?

Outside, a heavy drizzle fell from the dark gray sky. Darling wasn't known for its great weather any time of year, but since Hunter had left five days ago, the island seemed permanently under a rain cloud. It suited her state of mind.

She had been avoiding Vivian. Last night, Grace had eaten pasta sauce straight from a bowl like soup just to skip going to the grocery store. It was a silly thing to do. Vivian was her friend. But the only thing Grace wanted right now was to be left alone with her bad mood.

Grace stood at the sink and reached for a mug from the dish bin, but it slipped from her soapy hand. With a crash, the mug splintered into a hundred ceramic shards that flew every which way across the wood floor.

Cursing under her breath, Grace looked at Ruby. The last thing she wanted was for the little dog to cut her feet. "Stay."

She dried her hands on her apron and grabbed a broom, quickly sweeping up the pieces. Not only was Grace in a bad mood the past few days, but it felt like she couldn't do anything right either. She had accidentally mixed up the decaf and the regular, something she had luckily realized before serving anyone for the day. Grace couldn't get the crema right on her espresso. She had burned countless croissants. Now, the mug.

Grace dumped the dustpan into the trash. "I should rename this place Butterfinger Bistro."

The worst mistake was telling him to leave.

Her heart ached. Sometimes it felt like Hunter had cursed her. He came here with his dimple and his gray eyes and smiled his way back into her heart. He made her want things she had convinced herself she didn't want anymore. Hunter helped her learn to dream again, and then he left her with nightmares.

Every day, she hoped to hear something from him. Every day, she was disappointed.

Grace had resumed her old routine, hoping that it would provide some comfort. She and Ruby kept their afternoon walks. Grace planned to go for a hike on Sunday and had ordered a new romance book online as a treat. She was back to making dinner for one.

But instead of comforting her, the routine seemed to

shine a light on everything that was wrong in her life. Grace had spent the last two years telling herself that she was better off alone. But was that the truth?

Her stomach growled. Like her emotions, her appetite had been all over the place the past few days. The scale told her she was down three pounds. Heartbreak was the best diet she had ever tried.

Grace warmed up a croissant and cut it in half, slathering the flaky pastry with chocolate hazelnut spread. It was one of her favorite treats, one that she rarely allowed herself. But the indulgent snack was tasteless.

With a groan, she rested her head in her hands. Grace was past caring about things getting back to normal. She would settle for just okay.

Ruby whined and circled around her, begging for her own taste of the snack.

"Sorry, girl. You can't have chocolate." Grace forced herself to at least finish half of her food before covering the other half in plastic. Maybe she would have the rest later.

Her shoulders sagged. Another lie. She should save herself the trouble and put it in the garbage now.

Grace checked the time. The clock was moving as slowly as the fat yellow slugs that were found on the island. Hunter really had sucked all the fun out of life when he left Darling.

She tidied up, wiping down tables that were already clean and washing the few dishes left from the day so far. She saved the sweeping and mopping for later.

Grace eyed the bookshelves. Maybe a good story would distract her. She was perusing her collection for something to read when the bell over the door chimed. She forced a smile before turning around. Her personal problems had nothing to do with her business. But her current customer was the last person she expected. "Oh, hello."

Natasha smiled back at her. "I hope I'm not disturbing you. But weather like this calls for hot chocolate."

"Of course you're not disturbing me. That's what I'm here for." Grace stepped behind the counter. She had gone two years without meeting Natasha. Now, the mystic had come by twice in one month. The world really was on its head. "Did you want a double fudge cookie too? Warmed up?"

"You have a good memory." Natasha's blue eyes twinkled. "Must be torture."

Grace added milk to the frothing tin. How true those words were. "Something like that."

The roar of the steaming wand filled the coffee shop. Once the milk was hot, Grace whisked it into a mug with hot chocolate mix. After topping the drink with a healthy dose of whipped cream and chocolate shavings, she passed the mug to Natasha. "Let me get that cookie for you."

Natasha's delicate brows squished together. "Oh no. I forgot to bring my mug back from last time."

Grace lifted a shoulder. Most of the time, people remembered. When they didn't, it wasn't the end of the world. She had worked a few missing mugs into the yearly budget. "Maybe next time."

"I bet you wouldn't forget. Not with that memory of yours."

Grace handed Natasha the cookie in a paper sleeve. "It's not perfect."

"No, nothing is. That's why I am glad I don't remember it all."

Grace's throat grew tight. If only she could pick and choose what she remembered. "Some things are impossible to forget."

"And some things are impossible to remember." Natasha lifted her mug. "Like Darling before the Driftwood."

Grace shrugged. "It's easy to please when you're the only coffee shop in town."

"People don't come here for the coffee, Grace. They come here for you."

She swallowed. "That doesn't mean they need me."

Natasha's blue gaze held hers. "Funny how sometimes we don't even realize we want something, but once we have it, we realize how perfect it truly is."

Grace's nose burned. Like her life in Darling. Like being with Hunter again.

"I won't forget to bring my cup back next time." Natasha glanced over her shoulder as she stepped outside. "Though these things have a way of working out for the best. After all, leaving something behind is the perfect excuse to come back."

Once the door closed behind Natasha, Grace set the bell on the counter. Blinking furiously, she took refuge in the storeroom. The only thing more embarrassing than crying would be someone seeing her lose it.

Her breath was ragged as hot tears spilled over. Even though Natasha's message had been cryptic, she saw the truth in the older woman's words.

It had nothing to do with the coffee shop and everything to do with what was in Grace's heart.

Grace wiped at her eyes. She had it all wrong this whole time. She had thought she had contributed something to Darling by opening the coffee shop. But it was Grace that the town loved. It was she that they supported with their cappuccinos and cherry danishes. Darling could've survived a hundred years without the Driftwood Coffee Company. But they wanted her here.

Did that mean Grace was wrong about Hunter too?

What if you already have everything you ever wanted?

Grace looked around at the place that had been such a

haven, and now it felt so empty. All these years, she had resented Hunter for not giving her the home she craved. But what was a home without the man she loved?

She took a shaky breath. No one was going to rescue her. No one would ride down Main Street on a white horse. No one would climb up to her window and carry her away.

Grace squared her shoulders. But who needed a hero? She had rescued herself once before. She could do it again. And she knew exactly where to start.

She had to find Hunter.

Grace wouldn't admit it to a soul, but she had checked his social media last night. Based on his photos, he was still in Sedona.

She grabbed her laptop and pulled up the airline website. Ruby whined and rested her small head on her lap. Grace dug her fingers into the dog's soft fur. "I'll be back soon."

Once she had her flight picked out, she keyed in her credit card number. The page refreshed with a confirmation number. For the first time since Hunter left, the knot in her stomach loosened.

Grace smiled to herself. Maybe this was all one big mistake. But it was better to make a mistake than to do nothing at all.

CHAPTER TWENTY-SIX

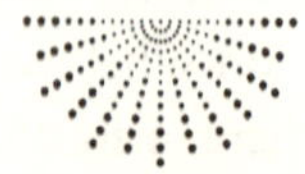

HUNTER

It would've been easier if he wasn't such a coward. Hunter could've caught a flight with Mac, reaching Darling much faster than with the ferry. But a declaration of love was embarrassing enough without witnesses.

Once docked in Darling, it took everything Hunter had to not run all the way to the Driftwood. After the drive to Phoenix and the flight to Seattle, he was champing at the bit to talk to Grace. Everything seemed like an obstacle between him and where he wanted to be.

He stepped off the ferry, walking into town as raindrops smacked against his jacket. Already, his shoulders felt lighter. After a week away, there was something comforting about being back in Darling. Same old colorful buildings. Same rusty cars. Same gray sky.

Hunter took a deep breath, inhaling the salty sea air. It felt like coming home.

The closer he got to the coffee shop, the faster he walked. Luckily, he didn't see anyone on his way there. Hunter wasn't ready to answer questions. He wasn't even sure he understood himself these days.

When he'd first come to Darling, it was supposed to be temporary. He had only wanted to get away from the pressures of the real world. After losing Jack and Aunt Linda, it seemed like all the joy had been sucked right out of life. Hunter had thought he would never feel okay again.

Before he had first shown up in the small town, the idea of being back with Grace, of giving her everything she wanted, of turning his life upside down in order to do so, was so wild that he couldn't even have imagined it.

What an idiot he had been.

He turned the corner, walking up Main Street. All the more reason he should've never left Darling six days ago. So what if they had a stupid fight? Shouldn't he know from his career, from all he had been through in life, that nothing worthwhile came easy? It was often those things, those complicated and challenging things, that made life worth living.

And life without Grace wasn't any kind of life at all.

The coffee shop came into view, and his heart fluttered. Hunter stepped in front of the door, smiling so big that his cheeks hurt. He couldn't wait to see the look on Grace's face when he walked in. Hopefully, she didn't immediately throw him out on his ass.

His apology sat on the tip of his tongue. Hunter was ready to tell Grace everything he should've told her a long time ago. Even if it wasn't good enough, at least she would know how much he truly loved her.

Hunter pulled on the door, but it didn't budge. He gave it another tug, harder this time. He frowned. Was it stuck?

He glanced to the side, and his stomach sank. The *Open* sign was dark.

Hunter cupped his hands and peered inside. Lights off. Tables empty. No sign of Grace or Ruby.

Inching his way along the windows, he looked for any clue as to what was going on. Grace never closed down on a weekday. Had something happened?

"She's gone," an accented voice said behind him.

Hunter turned, his eyebrows climbing up his forehead when he spotted Natasha. She didn't look the least bit surprised to see him, however. Popping up out of nowhere seemed to be her MO. Maybe she *was* gifted. "Grace is gone? Gone where?"

"Ah. That's a good question."

Hunter ran a hand over his face. "I'm an idiot."

"Things change. That includes people's minds."

"What are you saying?"

"What I am saying is it's not too late."

Hunter's head throbbed as fatigue and frustration mixed together. Even if he did know where to find Grace, how was he supposed to come back from this? He had his chance, multiple chances, and one by one, he had blown them all. "Well, what if I go after her and she tosses me out on my ass? Or what if she says yes, but it turns out I can't deal with life in Darling? I can't give up my photography, and she won't leave this place."

"You know the answer, Hunter. You always have." Natasha tapped on her chest, directly over her heart. "It's right here."

His throat tightened. No wonder Natasha gave him the heebie-jeebies. Sometimes the truth was the scariest thing of all.

Hunter's phone buzzed, and he reached for it. In some delusional part of his brain, he hoped it was Grace. But the call was from Dana. He didn't bother to answer, shoving the phone back into his pocket. He knew she was hoping for good news, and he didn't have it. "Sorry. Work."

"I understand. I'll see you when you get back."

"Get back?"

"From finding Grace, of course." Natasha turned and walked away.

The weight of the world pressed down on him, and suddenly, it was all so overwhelming. He lowered himself to a seat on the steps in front of the coffee shop.

Hunter rested his head in his hands. Where the heck *was* Grace? When would she be back? Did she have Ruby with her?

Dammit, he missed that little dog. Hunter could almost hear the tap of her nails, smell the damp dog stink after they took a walk in the rain. He pressed the heels of his hands into his eyes, determined not to blubber like a baby in the middle of Main Street.

Hunter frowned. Weird. He could feel the dog nudging his leg. He lifted his head, blinking. "Ruby?"

She sat, looking up at him with bright blue eyes.

Hunter's heart skipped a beat. If Ruby was nearby, then Grace had to be too. He looked to the side, his shoulders sagging when he saw Vivian standing there instead of his wife. "Where's Grace?"

"She isn't here. I'm just dog-sitting."

"Shit. I need to talk to her. I need to tell her I'm an idiot."

The corner of Vivian's mouth lifted. "I see you've perfected your apology speech already."

Ruby nuzzled Hunter, and he dug his hand into her fluffy coat. Grace had to be back soon. Hunter couldn't imagine she'd leave Ruby behind for long.

His phone vibrated. Probably Dana again. But he wasn't in the mood to talk. He pulled out his phone to send the call to voicemail.

Hunter nearly dropped the device when he saw Grace's name flashing on the screen. "Grace?"

"Hunter! Where are you?"

"I wanted to ask you the same thing. I'm in Darling."

"In Alaska?"

He smiled. "It's the only Darling I know of."

She let out a huff. "We're quite the pair. I'm in Sedona."

"But how did you know I was still there?"

"I looked up your social media. I wanted to see you again, to talk to you. Hunter, I'm sorry I told you to go—"

"No," he interrupted. "I want to have this conversation face-to-face."

"If only both of us didn't get the same idea. Great minds and all that."

"What are the odds? I'm the one who came back, and you're the one who went on an adventure."

Grace barked a laugh. "I can't decide if that means we're meant to be or doomed not to."

Hunter cleared his throat. He wasn't going to waste another minute. He only had time for the truth. That's what Grace deserved too. "So, what do you want? Which one of us stays?"

"Neither. Let's meet where it started."

Hunter rubbed his forehead with his free hand. "Do you mean what I think you mean?"

"Mm-hmm. See you there. I'll text you when my flight lands."

Hunter ended the call and turned to Vivian. "Do you mind dog-sitting for just a bit longer?"

She grinned. "Not at all."

Hunter called Dana back and asked her to arrange another flight.

Dana let out a whistle. "I gotta hand it to you, kid. You do adventure like no one else. One-way ticket? Any idea where you're going after?"

He chewed on the inside of his cheek. Hunter had spent a lifetime looking forward to the next place, always passing through. In his mind, he had places to go and nowhere to be.

Except he did have somewhere to be. Or someone to be with. He should've been with Grace. All these years, she was the one who truly mattered. The one who made all those places special. The one with whom each memory was one worth remembering.

He smiled, his heart full. "Just one-way."

Hunter slipped the phone back into his pocket and stood.

"What's the plan?" Vivian asked.

He squared his shoulders. He couldn't get back the two years he and Grace had spent apart. Hunter couldn't rip up the divorce papers to keep their marriage intact. He couldn't go back in time and tell her to delete the dating app.

But he could do *something*.

Grace lived vicariously through romance books. Now, Hunter was going to help her live one for real.

CHAPTER TWENTY-SEVEN

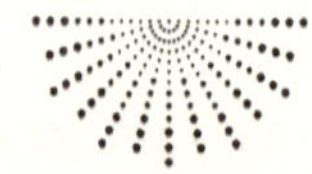

GRACE

Grace's hand shook as she set down the coffee cup. She should've ordered decaf.

She blinked, her eyes gritty. People rushed around her, shuffling between arrivals and departures, pickups and drop-offs.

Grace had gotten to Vegas yesterday and checked into a cheap room on the Strip, knowing Hunter's flight wouldn't land until the next morning. She had felt ridiculous, leaving Sedona the minute she got there. People traveled from all over the world to see the iconic red rock landscape. But Grace was a woman on a mission.

It had been years since she'd been in Vegas. After being in Alaska and detoxing from the modern world, it was a shock to the system. She had walked the Strip for an hour, trying to find something to eat. Grace had finally accepted that she didn't have an appetite. After sipping on a margarita at the hotel bar, she had gone back to her room, hoping the booze would knock her out.

Instead, she had tossed and turned, checking the time each hour. Grace's plan had been to talk to Hunter calmly. She didn't want to get emotional about it. She didn't want to have unreasonable expectations. But exhaustion and anticipation kicked that plan to the curb.

Now, she would settle for not being a complete and total mess when she saw him. Even that would be a stretch.

Grace fidgeted with the stirring stick. Doubt whispered in her ear again, but she shoved it away. She had lived with questions for too long.

She checked the time. His flight should arrive any moment.

Feeling light-headed, Grace closed her eyes. She needed sleep.

She snapped her eyes open again. She needed answers.

It was ironic that they'd ended up in Vegas. Life was funny that way. Vegas was where they had met. It was where they had gotten married one night, the same day that Hunter had suggested it.

Grace had dreamed of a huge wedding, followed by an around-the-world honeymoon. But even if they had taken the time to plan something like that, it wasn't in the cards for two broke kids, one in college and one who hadn't bothered. They didn't even have the money for rings, and in the end, they'd never gotten around to getting them.

She smiled at the memory of how much fun they had that night all the same. Hunter had promised he would give her a lifetime of honeymoons to make up for their simple wedding. And hadn't he?

Her heart squeezed. Hunter had kept every promise he had ever made, including his wedding vows.

All these years, Grace had blamed him for falling short, for depriving her of what she wanted. But Hunter hadn't failed her. She had failed herself.

Grace had never asked for what she truly wanted. She had been too afraid to have it.

The sliding doors of the arrivals gate opened again, another flight disembarking. Grace searched the crowd, but there was still no sign of Hunter.

She dropped her gaze to the plastic tabletop, her coffee half-finished. Grace set the cup aside. Nothing was going to help her with exhaustion at this point, and it was only making her jitters worse.

Because as eager as Grace was to see Hunter, she was equally scared that he wouldn't show. It was a long way between Darling and Las Vegas. Plenty of time to change his mind. Plenty of time to realize he was better off without her holding him back.

Stop that.

The doors opened again, sending a whoosh of air across the room as the passengers poured out into the terminal.

Her heart climbed into her throat. There, at the front of the crowd, was a redhead with gray eyes taking long strides towards her.

"I'm pretty sure you just tripped that guy," Grace teased as Hunter walked up.

"Did I? Didn't even notice." He leaned down, kissing her deeply. If Grace had thought she was light-headed before, she had another thing coming.

She gasped as he pulled away, the world spinning.

Hunter searched her eyes. "I wanted one more kiss. Just in case."

"In case of what?"

"In case you changed your mind. I know I can't expect you to forgive me, no matter how much I want it."

Her throat tightened. They really were two of a kind. A perfect pair. "No, Hunter. I spent so much time holding myself back, too scared to ask for what I wanted. Then I blamed you for not giving it to me. Can you forgive *me*?"

He took her hands in his. "Counteroffer: let's forgive ourselves. For being two idiots in love who almost messed that up."

"Do you mean—"

Hunter pulled her close, wrapping his arms around her. "I really hadn't thought this conversation would happen at the domestic arrivals gate, but I'm not missing my chance again. I love you, Grace. Always have. Always will. I'll spend a lifetime proving that to you. I know I can't expect another chance, but God, I would love one."

Her heart nearly burst from her chest. How could she have ever for a moment doubted this man? There was just one problem. "But our divorce is finalized as of tomorrow, remember? Today is the last day we're married."

"Honey, you're in luck." He stepped back and set his backpack on the ground, unzipping a pocket. Hunter pulled out an envelope and handed it to Grace.

She opened it, slipping out the paperwork. "Our divorce papers?"

"Yep. I had Dana get them for me."

Grace shook her head. "She really does organize your whole life, huh?"

"I have no problem admitting it."

"But why did you want to show me these? I have my own copy, you know." Grace quirked up the corner of her mouth. "For a while, I even considered framing them."

"I'd be disappointed if you didn't." He chuckled. "Hold on. They'll make sense in a minute."

Hunter reached back into his bag, pulling out something small enough to fit in his fist.

Before Grace could stop him, he lowered himself to one

knee. People paused to gawk, whispering to each other as they pointed at Grace and Hunter.

Her underarms prickled with sweat, and Grace reached for his arm, trying to pull him to his feet. "Hunter, please."

He didn't budge. "I know you hate attention. But I refuse to not show the world how much you mean to me."

She gulped and let go. Wasn't this exactly what had been the problem before? Why not let Hunter love her as much as he could? The only one stopping him was Grace.

"I know you don't like flashy things. But I owe you a wedding ring." He opened up the box.

Grace frowned. Nothing. There was nothing there. She looked up at Hunter. "I don't get it."

"I want to pick out our rings together because I want the rest of our lives to be what we both want. Because you see, the only thing I really want is you. Grace Hart, will you please be my wife again and stay my wife this time?"

She hadn't even realized she was crying until she tasted the salty tears. This was better than any romance book she'd ever read. No hero could compare to the man in front of her. "Yes. Yes, I'll marry you. Again."

With a whoop, Hunter stood and kissed her, waterworks and all. "Good thing we have those divorce papers, huh?"

She sniffed, wiping at her eyes with the back of her hand. "Why?"

"So we can get married again tomorrow. Then we never have to go a single day divorced."

Grace's heart swelled. Just when she thought she couldn't love him more. "Then I guess it's a good thing we're in Vegas. We can have the same cheesy chapel wedding we did all those years ago."

"Unless—"

"Unless what?"

"Dana is a fairy godmother."

Grace let out a laugh. "She *really* does it all, doesn't she?"

"Hey. She's got to keep her best client happy." Hunter grabbed his suitcase with one hand and Grace's hand with the other. "Now, come on, let's go get ready. We have a wedding tomorrow."

Grace gave him a gentle nudge. "Just don't think you can combine my birthday present and anniversary present from now on. I'm going to expect two gifts. Nice ones."

They made their way back to the hotel where Grace was staying. After adding Hunter's name to the reservation and dropping off his bag, they struck out on another adventure. First, they found Grace a dress in the same pink color that she had worn for her birthday. Not exactly a conventional choice, but she joked that a traditional wedding outfit in Darling was a flannel shirt and rubber boots. Then, after picking out rings, they had an early dinner before heading back to the hotel.

Grace had thought she wouldn't be able to sleep again and was surprised to wake up the next morning feeling rested. Doubt had left her, leaving only calm certainty.

They had brunch and a couple of mimosas—it was Vegas, after all—before heading to the chapel. A limo shuttled them around, something they could've never afforded the first time they had gotten married.

As they stood in front of the officiant, it was impossible for Grace not to compare this wedding to their first one. They had been in love, with the world at their feet and life stretching before them. Grace had thought it was the happiest day of her life.

She had been wrong. Standing across from Hunter at the same chapel with seventeen years passed between them, Grace realized she felt even happier than before. Even more hopeful. Even more in love.

They still had so many years, so much time ahead of

them, to enjoy life together. All of the happiest moments were yet to come.

If someone had told Grace that Hunter would show up at her coffee shop only a month ago, she would've laughed. If someone had told her she would marry him again, she would've called that person crazy.

But what was crazy was telling herself that she didn't love him. What was crazy was blaming him for everything when she was just as responsible. What was crazy was that she almost missed out on spending the rest of her life with this amazing man.

Hunter put his arm around her as they walked out of the chapel into the bright Las Vegas sunshine. "How can I make your dreams come true today, my wife?"

She giggled. "God, you're cheesy."

"Cheesy, you say? What do you prefer? Romance? Tough guy? You tell me. I want to do whatever it takes to make you happy."

Grace bumped him softly with her shoulder. "I prefer we enjoy this trip. I'm not you. I don't get vacations very often."

"Yeah? Well, you didn't have a problem finding a dog-sitter."

"Vivian is a godsend. She's always offered, but I think she was shocked when I actually took her up on it. She said I should let her have Ruby since she's the only single person in town now."

Hunter waggled his eyebrows. "Hmm, Ruby as a magic talisman. I can see it."

Grace swallowed, giving Hunter a sideways glance. "Speaking of going back, I suppose this is closing the barn door after the horses are out, but what exactly are you going to do?"

"About what?" He took her hand as they turned the corner to

head back to the limo. They had dinner reservations that night, five-star dining overlooking the Strip. Hunter had thought of it all. He wasn't much of a planner, but when he did plan, he pulled out all the stops. Even if he had needed Dana's help.

"About your work. I really don't want to leave the coffee shop, and you can't be a world-famous photographer working only from Darling."

"Ah, I understand now. I've got it all figured out, don't you worry." He squeezed her hand before opening the car door for her.

She scooted into the limo. "I won't worry. Once you tell me what the plan is."

Hunter climbed in behind her. "Remember that creative director job? The one in New York?"

Grace's heart sank, but she immediately tried to shake it off. She refused to feel sad. Not on her wedding day. She wanted to enjoy it to the fullest. After all, she didn't plan on having another one ever again. "So you'll be on the East Coast. Long distance, then."

"Yes to the job. No to the East Coast."

She knit her brows together. "How?"

"Dana strikes again." Hunter reached for the champagne that sat in an ice bucket, pouring a glass. "I'll work remotely, most of the time. There is nothing I can't do with a good internet connection. Though we may have to occasionally take trips to the East Coast. And maybe some trips for fun too."

She bit her lip as he passed her the flute glass. "Are you sure? I thought you were allergic to staying in one place too long."

"It turns out the only thing I am allergic to is being away from you. The rest we can figure out along the way. Now, can we please start the fun stuff?" Hunter poured himself a drink and held up his glass. "To love, the greatest adventure of all."

Grace clinked her glass to his, taking a sip of the bubbly drink.

Her heart stretched in her chest. Just when she thought she'd had enough of adventure, she was starting again.

EPILOGUE

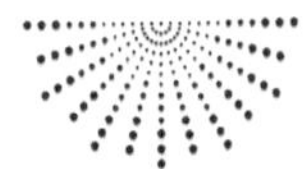

GRACE

Six months.

Six months since Hunter had stepped into the Driftwood Coffee Company and given Grace the surprise of her life.

"You know what's the craziest thing about this year?" Grace rested her elbows on the bistro table.

Hunter stood in front of the espresso machine. He finished pulling the shots, pouring them into mugs, and adding hot water to each one. "What's that?"

"This is the longest I've ever known you to stay in one place."

Hunter carried their drinks over, setting the two Americanos down on the table. "Hey, I had a home as a kid."

"I mean since I've met you. You used to get antsy after a week." Grace took a careful sip of her drink. "Damn. Giving me a run for my money."

"I don't need your pity." Hunter tried his own coffee, his eyes widening. "Never mind. This is amazing. Step aside for the real barista."

Grace chuckled as she glanced at her smartwatch. Fifteen minutes until the Driftwood opened for the day. Or at least fifteen minutes until she turned on the hot pink *Open* sign. Darling was pretty easygoing when it came to business hours. If the lights were on and Grace was downstairs, then the locals considered it fair game to knock on the door. Not that she ever turned anyone away. No, Grace understood what it was to need a beacon in the dark. "You don't have to get up with me this early, you know. You can sleep in."

"I think all the time changes and crappy flight connections are ingrained into my biology now. I couldn't sleep if I tried. Although it might help if you stayed in bed with me." Hunter winked.

Her face grew warm, and she held up a finger. "No flirting before five in the morning."

"What? Why?"

"Because. We're in our forties. We're not teenagers."

He puffed his chest out. "Almost forty, thank you very much. And not dead. Plenty of life in us yet, sweetheart."

Grace shifted in her seat. She told the guilt to go away. She asked the words not to come out of her mouth, afraid of what the answer would be. "Do you miss it? Traveling all the time?"

He shrugged, taking another sip of coffee. "I still travel. We're going to New York next week."

She nodded. Hunter had some work meetings that he wanted to attend in person, and they planned to combine it with celebrating his fortieth birthday in style.

Grace didn't mind the trips to New York. She particularly enjoyed scouring all the independent bookstores to fill the bookshelves at their condo there. And though it wasn't even Thanksgiving yet, she was looking forward to seeing all the gorgeous Christmas decorations that covered the city already.

Luckily, Grace was able to take all the time she needed when they traveled out of town. They took Ruby with them, and Grace had help at the coffee shop now. Once word got out that she was looking to hire a few people to cover the Driftwood on an as-needed basis, a local put Grace in touch with his two teenage nephews in Ketchikan. The kids were glad for the work and were familiar with Darling.

It all made perfect sense. Grace couldn't think of a better arrangement. But that didn't stop her voice from cracking when she spoke again. "Not as much as you used to."

"Oh, sweetheart." Hunter stood and pulled Grace up into a hug. "I'm not going anywhere. Did I enjoy my time on the road? You know I did. But people can do lots in a lifetime. And lots doesn't interest me anyway. There is a tall, gorgeous brunette who has my entire focus."

Her heart skipped a beat as her gaze roamed across his familiar face. His gray eyes. The faint freckles. That damn dimple. After almost twenty years, he still took her breath away. "I know you love traveling. That's who you are, Hunter."

Hunter gave her a squeeze. "I love you more. Although it would've been easier for us if I could've figured that out sooner. Then we wouldn't have had to get divorced and remarried in the same year, huh?"

"But it wouldn't have been nearly as interesting." Grace pressed a kiss to his lips before stepping away. "Showtime."

"And that's my cue to get out of your hair." Hunter grabbed his coffee and headed upstairs. He usually got to work around the same time she did. The early start worked well for his team on the East Coast, and it meant he was free to spend afternoons with Grace.

Despite being in the middle of nowhere, they always found a way to have fun together. They had been hiking a lot lately. At this rate, Grace was going to be in better shape at forty than she was at twenty. Hunter always brought along his camera, of course, and enjoyed taking photos just for the fun of it.

She flicked on the *Open* sign at the same moment that Mac stepped inside the coffee shop. Grace fixed his pour-over and handed him the drink. Mac was a man of few words on a good day, but he hadn't uttered so much as a peep this morning. "Everything okay?"

Then Mac did something so unexpected, so wild, that Grace almost fainted and smacked her head on the imported Italian espresso machine.

Mac smiled. "Just thinking it's nice that you stuck around."

"Stuck around?" she parroted, still gathering her senses.

"Yep. We're finally in the safe zone. When you first opened for business, I was worried you'd get your fill of Darling real quick. Then after your husband showed up, I thought you were about to abandon this place and leave us clutching our instant coffee."

"Then you don't know me."

Mac snorted. "You? You weren't my clue, Sherlock. It was that photographer upstairs." He shook his head. "Take it from one sucker to another. I know when a man has been ruined by a woman. Saddest shit I've ever seen."

Grace bit back a smile. "What does Hunter have to do with me leaving or staying?"

Mac rolled his eyes. "Isn't it obvious? A woman is the only one smart enough to figure it out."

With a grumble, he grabbed his coffee cup and pushed open the door.

Grace shook her head. Maverick Carter, the least likely feminist in the world. Or at least Alaska.

As usual, Mac kicked off the start of a busy day at the Driftwood Coffee Company. Grace used to wonder what they had done before her. Now, she wondered what she had done before them.

Hours flew by as she steamed milk, pulled shots of espresso, and whisked hot chocolate. There wasn't a pastry left in the display case by one in the afternoon.

The first to sell out were the new varieties that Hunter had suggested adding to the menu. She joked that he was good for business. Nice to look at, famous, and great taste in pastry. He told her that's why she fell for him in the first place.

Throughout the day, Grace kept a lookout for Vivian, but her friend never made an appearance. Every time Vivian dropped off an order, Grace asked her to stay and have a cup of tea. When Grace went to the store to go grocery shopping, she would ask if Vivian wanted to get a drink at the Buck.

But Vivian always insisted three was a crowd. She still offered to dog-sit, joking that she was the only single person in town left to do so.

Grace had told her they would see about that. This town had some kind of magic.

After turning off the *Open* sign, Grace had just started cleaning out the espresso machine when Hunter popped his head into the shop. "Closing up?"

"You don't have to help me. I've got this."

"But I want to help you." He tackled the pile of dirty dishes first. Then he cleaned out the sink and tied off the trash bags. "I'll take these outside."

Grace watched him heave the bags up, his shirtsleeves straining against his rounded biceps.

She practically had to fan herself with a menu. Was it hilarious or romantic that she got turned on watching him do chores? Oh, who cared? It was her life and no one else's.

Hunter came back inside and washed his hands. "What are you in the mood for tonight?"

You.

Grace smiled. "Any suggestions?"

Ruby let out a yap and sat by the door.

Hunter raised an eyebrow. "I think the dog just made a plan."

Grace laughed as she slipped on a coat and clipped on Ruby's leash. "I'll be back in about thirty minutes."

"Now, just hold on. You think I don't want to come with you? I live for potty walks."

She held the door open for him. "Hmm, that would make a nice bumper sticker. But you don't have a car. Tattoo, maybe?"

"Hell no. You know that would ruin my natural beauty."

Grace giggled as the three of them walked outside. They strolled down to the beach, their shoes crunching against the rocky soil.

Once off the leash, Ruby ran around like a maniac, snapping at the waves and getting soaked.

"Maybe next time, consider a short-hair dog," Hunter observed.

"You can't tell me you don't love the wet-dog smell?"

He made a face. "I love you. I love photography. But I do not love wet-dog smell."

She whistled, and Ruby trotted back over to them. Grace clipped on the leash again. "In that case, I'll do the honor of drying her off when we get home."

As soon as they were back, Hunter snatched the towel from Grace, working it over Ruby's fur.

Grace fought a smile. "I thought you hated wet-dog smell?"

"Guess I love the damn dog more," he muttered.

They fixed dinner for two and opened a bottle of wine. Taking their time, they chatted about her day at the coffee shop and how his work was going as they enjoyed the risotto.

Once they had cleaned up from dinner, they made their way to the living room. Grace sat in her chair, book in hand. Hunter balanced his laptop on his legs as he sat on the couch. Soft snores came from Ruby's dog bed.

After trying to read the same page at least three times, Grace finally gave up and set her book down. She picked up her glass of wine, looking at Hunter.

His eyes moved back and forth as he focused on the screen. She knew he was a million miles away. It used to drive her crazy. She would wonder if he even cared about her.

But Grace understood that his work was part of his soul. Part of what made him the man she loved.

She smiled to herself. And married twice.

Hunter looked up from his laptop. "What's so funny?"

"Nothing. Just thinking."

He gestured towards her book. "Not that interesting, huh?"

"It's fine. Just not in the mood to read right now, I suppose."

He raised an eyebrow. "Do you need a medevac? I can only assume something is terribly wrong. You are always in the mood to read."

"Nothing is wrong. Actually, everything is very, very right."

"Oh yeah? How so?"

She sipped her wine. Grace still loved reading, but she wasn't searching for something in her stories anymore. She didn't escape from the world in romance books, only to compare them to her life and find it lacking.

What if you already have everything you ever wanted?

Natasha had been right. Vivian had known it too. Even

Mac's mysterious comment from this morning suddenly made sense.

When Grace had walked away from Hunter and moved to the middle of nowhere, she had thought she had nothing left. But as it turned out, she had gained everything.

Grace had a home. She had friends and a community. She had found purpose in the coffee shop and getting to know the locals in Darling. Even Hunter had found his way back into her life.

Yes, they had both had to make compromises. It wasn't fair to force one to live in the other's world all the time. But it was worth it. Life was so much better with Hunter in it.

Her gaze wandered to the wedding photo that hung on the wall. For now, it was the only picture there. But it was a start. Grace wanted to cover her apartment in photos, remembering each precious and necessary moment.

Grace smiled at her husband, her heart full. "I just realized that real life is better than any romance book."

After all, Hunter had said it himself. Love was the greatest adventure of all.

* * *

A NOTE FROM THE AUTHOR

Thank you for taking the time to read my book. I hope you had as much fun reading it as I did writing it.

If you did enjoy it, and want to help other people discover Grace and Hunter's story, please consider leaving a review at the retailer where you purchased this book. It would absolutely make my day (especially if share who your favorite character is!).

Thank you kindly.

ACKNOWLEDGMENTS

Given carte blanche, I could turn this section into a novel of its own. But then the book would be really heavy to hold, so I'll try to control myself.

To Sarah, for once again making everything better. Thank you for helping Grace and Hunter be all they could be.

To Sandra, for the perfect final polish! Your proofreading skills are unrivaled.

To the team at Best Page Forward, for another beautiful cover and delightful description. A special shout out to TNae, who probably needed a tequila shot every time my name popped up in her inbox. Your patience and kindness are much appreciated.

To my mom, who talked me through yet another book. I could not, would not do this without you.

To Mama, who was so good at being herself. You were a complete original, and sometimes I think people didn't knew what to do with that.

Thank you all.

ABOUT THE AUTHOR

Lark Holiday is the author of feel-good and funny romances. She lives in California with her opinionated dogs and her human family. When she's not writing, she spends her time going for walks, vacuuming dog hair, and feeling like she should probably be writing.

Though Lark is based in California now, she lived in Alaska many times over the past few decades. Her time in The Last Frontier inspired the Darling Men series.

www.ingramcontent.com/pod-product-compliance
Lightning Source LLC
Chambersburg PA
CBHW021414010826
48972CB00014B/2282